THE
HALF-LIFE
OF PLANETS

THE HALF-LIFE
OF PLANETS

 A novel by Emily Franklin & Brendan Halpin

Hyperion

New York

Thanks to—

My co-author . . . and Faye Bender, Tamson Weston, and everyone at Disney • Hyperion, AJS and the off-spring, those boys of summer long ago, the musicians mentioned herein, my brothers for sharing their music with me, and my parents for letting me be the family DJ —EF

Emily Franklin. Douglass Stewart. Suzanne Demarco, Casey Nelson, Rowen Halpin, Kylie Nelson, Squeeze, Hank Williams (I and III), The Kinks, and Kiss —BH

Text copyright © 2010 by Emily Franklin and Brendan Halpin

Printed in United States of America

First Edition

10 9 8 7 6 5 4 3 2 1

V567-9638-5-10091

Library of Congress Cataloging-in-Publication Data on file.

Reinforced binding

ISBN 978-1-4231-2111-4

Visit www.hyperionteens.com

*To all those names on my list,
but most especially the last one*

—EF

*To Suzanne, co-star of my
favorite love story*

—BH

CHAPTER 1
LIANA

I am not a slut.

Evidence exists that is contrary to this statement, but this is what I'm thinking in the hospital bathroom. In movies, actors are always splashing water on their faces in times of crisis as if this will somehow explain to them what they should do. How they should feel. What comes next. I put my hands under the running water, chuck some of the tepid liquid up so it hits my cheeks and my forehead. All I feel is drenched.

I am not a slut. Even though I have a note in my pocket that suggests otherwise. Even though James Frenti, Pren Stevens, Mitchell Palmer, and Jett Alterman would beg to differ. Even though I could give a guided tour of all the different places I've kissed different boys in this semi-small town: the sand-gritty sidewalk near the fishing rocks, outside Sweet Nothings candy shop, under the stereotypical bleachers at school, in my own basement amid my parents' old records and my ancient kid drawings. Suffice it to say I am not an artist. I am also not a slut. Even though I could give this tour.

The Littered Kisses tour, I say to myself as though I'm a rock band. I look at my damp face, think about those kisses, about what it feels like to have someone's face that close to my own, how I can feel the warmth emanating from his skin. What it feels like to be that close to another person. I tug my T-shirt down so it covers my waist. This is more a nervous tic than a teenage-girl-hiding-her-body move, and definitely a habit I haven't been able to shake since I branded myself with a tattoo last summer. I run my thumb over the small circles, tug again at my shirt, and feel the note crumpled in my pocket, the four-letter word written on it tucked away.

I want to look at it now; to study it as I would a scientific document, weigh the possibilities (Is it true? What does it mean?), the mysteries (Who sent it? When? And why?). I want to evaluate it like I did in APS. Science is easy to understand. Even if it's complicated, I've always found it comforting. People get nervous about math, but the truth is, math is simple—there's correct and incorrect. And with science, you always know what you're trying to prove, you know your predictions. The order of science is a lullaby. Even the names—celestial mechanics, icy moons, star systems, brown dwarfs—provide everything you need, poetry to humor.

But Advanced Planetary Science, while it will dominate my summer and keep me trapped in the lab if I let it, has nothing to do with finding this note in my locker eight hours ago. Life is like that, though: one minute you're de-junking your locker—removing the old papers, stained T-shirts, AP Physics texts, *Worlds Apart: Black Holes and Space*, math tests, stray flip-flops, and CDs to get ready for summer—and the next minute you're holding in your hands a tiny slip of paper that changes everything. Or nothing. It depends how you look at it, which of course I haven't decided yet because I hardly had a chance to shove it in my pocket before coming here. I left the rest of my locker's contents outside in my beat-up brown Saab, but the lined piece of paper with exactly one word written on it is with me now. It's impossible to erase the looping script, the perfect *l* as though the word were "love" or something pleasant. This scientist I heard lecture last summer at the university basically said that it's possible to approach everything—food, shopping, dancing—with a scientific mind. For example, you could understand the physics of dancing—like some geeky girl in a movie who figures it out on paper and then suddenly can win some competition—or, presumably, science can just help you analyze anything. Even slut notes. Way back in basic bio we were taught that before you question what you have, you have to investigate how it got there. So I spend a few seconds wondering: Katie from homeroom, who glared at me when I came to class with a scarf around my neck in early June? Celeste, who is not celestial as her name implies but just bitchy and who liked Pren before I got to him? Who sends notes, and why, and did she—assuming it was a she—plan it out, or just rip off a corner from an old *Sound and the Fury* pop quiz and slip it in my locker on a whim? And then the truth, cold and plain as the metal bathroom shelf in front of me: it doesn't really matter who or why. Just that it exists.

So I know that geomorphology studies features on the planetary surface and reconstructs formational processes, and when this is applied to the note in my back pocket, I can deduce the following: the person who sent it wouldn't confront me directly, that the word itself is meant to hurt me, and that if I didn't think it was at all true, I wouldn't be standing here in the hospital bathroom, nervously thumbing the blue-and-purple tattoo on my hip. Saturn, turned on its side, a marbled moon in the distance behind it. As many mouths on mine as there have been, as many hands around my waist or tangled in my hair, no one has touched those circles. Maybe an accidental brushing, but no study of it, no examination of that surface. Slut.

I want to grab the note, but not with my wet hands. Instead I splash a little more water on my cheeks, press my dark bangs flat on my forehead, and wait for some giant revelation, like in the movies.

But unlike in the movies, I don't look placid and calm after this face-swim. I don't appear ready to take on the world. I just look the same.

I am not a slut. I swear I have proof. Proof I could provide if I get out of this hospital bathroom and back to the reality waiting outside the door.

Only the door opens, and in bursts—

"It's all over me!" The guy's about my age, maybe a little older; who can tell, really, because he's flustered and jumping around a little. It takes me only a few seconds to realize why:

his pants are soaking. And not just in any area. His crotch.

I look at him in the mirror, my green eyes focused on his—are they brown?—but he doesn't look back at me. He just stands there, flailing, unaware somehow that paper towels by the bushel are right in front of him.

"Here," I say when I can't take it any longer. I hate seeing people in need. Watching desperation spread like the liquid on his jeans makes my skin crawl—like those people who watch accidents, or stand by as a fight breaks out. So I help with what I can—in this case, paper towels. "There's more," I tell him, and tug my shirt over my tattoo. "Over by the door? See there's . . ."

But he doesn't see. He's caught up in the moment of blotting himself, and then suddenly, very suddenly, getting his bearings. "Oh, wait. Wait a second."

I nod, my arms crossed, the edges of my bangs still wet and plastered to my forehead. I blush for him. He must have just realized where he is. But he takes it well. He must be centered. Sure of himself. "It's okay," I tell him, and gesture to the bathroom. "It's the women's, but you know what?"

He doesn't answer. He doesn't look at me even though my eyes are glued to his face so I don't focus on his pants. "Squeeze!"

Now I'm confused until I see him looking at my chest and remember I'm wearing a concert shirt I took from one of those boxes in the basement. Next to the records are old stickers, programs, ticket stubs. "Gotta love Squeeze—*45's and Under*," I say, and he cracks up. "It's not that funny." He's got a deep laugh, calm too, which goes against

5

his flailing jumpy persona. Maybe he's not really an anxious person. Probably just surprised is all. But definitely able to hold his own in the least likely of places.

I could bolt now, run out of here as though it too is a stop on my tour—minus the kiss—but I don't. It seems right somehow that I should be stuck having some weird, random interaction in here while everything else is happening out there. Planets are spinning, diagnoses are being made, notes are being dropped into unsuspecting lockers. I chew on my lower lip.

"It's just, Squeeze, right? Famous song: 'Black Coffee in Bed.'" He mumbles a little here, his mouth stretched in a wide grin. He's older than I am, definitely. Only by a year or so, but how else to explain the fact that he's not particularly flustered by the lack of urinals? "'The stain on my notebook' . . . you know it, of course." I nod, because I do. I've memorized that whole album. "But now . . ." He laughs. "It's so stupid. I've got a stain on my pants and it's black."

Now I laugh, allow a quick glance, and shrug. "It *is* black. Why, is it coffee?" I can't think of any other stain that color. He takes his coffee black. Intense. I'm all about the milk and sugar. Not Splenda. Not skim milk. Creamy and truly sweet. But black-coffee drinkers who are under the age of twenty are all about intensity. Then I think of something besides coffee. "Is it ink?"

That's it. He's a writer. A writer who knows cool music. So maybe a musician. Which would be bad. At least for me, since drummers (James Frenti), guitarists (Mitchell Palmer), lead singers (Jett Alterman, Pren Stevens), even bass players get my heart racing. "So is it ink?" I ask again, wanting, not wanting.

He shakes his head, his wide shoulders back, his long-sleeved T-shirt pushed up to the elbows, a grin stretched across his mouth. "This is not black coffee in bed. It is not ink. It is Dark 'n' Daring."

I wrinkle my nose. A flaw in my thinking. "The energy drink?"

He shrugs and goes to the sink. "DnD," he says, and splashes water onto his pants, which doesn't help. In fact it's only making it worse, and I show this with my face, my eyebrows raised, but he still won't look at me. He's got that cool reserve. Not exactly aloof, but not all here either. "I don't even drink the stuff. But Chase does. All the time. I mean, like he might have an addiction. Like Jimmy Page. Or Steven Tyler before rehab. Chase will probably have to be weaned from the substance. Or no—go cold turkey and just one day go to the fridge and find that there are no more DnDs."

"I don't drink them either," I tell him, but the truth is I've never tried them. I don't want to ask who Chase is because I don't like to pry, and maybe it's some well-respected musician I'm supposed to know but don't. "I doubt I'd like Dark 'n' Darings anyway." I like root beer, preferably in a glass bottle, and that's it. At least, in terms of soda. If I can't have that, I won't have any. I can get pretty stuck in my ways.

"But, you know, he dared me."

"Who?" I try and get him to look at me by checking out his reflection in the long rectangle of mirror, but he's on his own time, blotting, splashing, thinking.

7

He turns to me now, the stain dark on his jeans, but the rest of him looking regular, like a guy I could see at school. Who I should see at school instead of in the bathroom at Westwood-Cranston General at the tail end of June, on what was the last day of classes. "Chase. Chase is always daring everyone to do everything. He's home from college for the summer, which would be fine—it was fine last year when we went to see Proverbial Nuance at the beach stage. But now he's back and—"

I hear footsteps outside and recognize them as my mother's. I have to go, I think, and then realize I need to say this aloud. I poke through my jeans at the planets on my hip and chew my lip. "I have to go."

He nods and shrugs, eyes me but at arm's length. Intense. I think that he'll ask where or why or thank me for the paper towels, or tell me why he's here, at the hospital too, but he doesn't. So I don't say anything else—not good-bye or anything—because really, is it necessary?

CHAPTER 2
HANK

The girl in the Squeeze shirt leaves me in the bathroom with a stain on my crotch. The stain on my notebook from "Black Coffee in Bed" was actually the second thing that popped into my mind when I saw her T-shirt.

When you see a girl with the word *Squeeze* written across her breasts, well, the band that gave us "Tempted," and, more importantly, "In Quintessence" is not the first thing that comes to mind. Even for me.

But I did not blurt out "Is that the band or just instructions?" because I paid attention to my surroundings and I tried to listen. I paused for a moment and realized that my surroundings were the ladies' room, where I wasn't supposed to be, which is actually just a men's room with a menstrual-supply dispenser on the wall and no urinals.

I've been trying to think about how other people might react to what I say. In this case, the other person was the girl with the breasts—well, they all have breasts, but few have breasts like this girl's breasts—might think that my barging into the ladies' room and making a breast joke meant that I was a weirdo.

I have some experience with people thinking I'm a weirdo. One day in seventh grade, a bunch of kids who used to threaten me for no reason that I could ever figure out decided to chant "Freak! Freak! Freak! Freak!" while pointing at me.

"The dance is called Le Freak, if you ever listened to the song, and while I appreciate the invitation, I'm not going to dance for you!"

They did not laugh at my joke, but neither did they continue their taunts. So, overall, I counted it as a successful interaction.

Of course, I wanted to explain to somebody how Chic, who recorded "Le Freak," also provided the music behind The Sugarhill Gang's "Rapper's Delight," though of course it was "Good Times" and not "Le Freak" that they were rapping over. But this would be pearls before swine as far as the middle school lunchroom taunters went.

I have had similar experiences with girls. Well, when I say I've had experiences with girls, I should make it clear that what I'm talking about are conversations. Or maybe not even that—I'm not sure what you call it when one person starts talking about a topic of interest only to find out the other person has no interest in that topic and walks away from the conversation. This is how most of my interactions with girls go.

Except for this one. She had a T-shirt, and despite the fact that she kept tugging on it, which stretched the word *Squeeze* even tighter across her breasts and also drew my eyes to her womanly hips, where her tugging hands were taking up residence, I managed to follow one of Allie's recommendations: *Find a common interest. Make a connection.* We had a conversation that, despite the location, felt fairly normal, or what I imagine normal to be.

Back to the bathroom, where I'm not supposed to be: I splash some water on my crotch and blot it with paper towels until at least the stain on my pants is just wet and not wet *and* black. I decide that the hand dryer might help me with the remaining wetness, so I hit the button and angle my hips toward the stream of hot air, trying to get it directly on my crotch.

This is when my mother walks in.

"Oh, Jesus Christ," she says. She puts her hand up to her forehead, and her Black Flag tattoo peeks out of the short-sleeved blouse she's wearing. "This is it, you know, this is really it. I mean, it's not like I'm having a good day already, and I walk into the *women's bathroom*—you do know you're in the women's bathroom?"

"Yes, I met a really nice girl in here who—"

"Humping the wall! Like you're a Jack Russell terrier or something! Honestly! I think you're making so much progress, and then I find you *here* doing *that*!"

Later my mom will cry and call me her sweet boy and tell me how much she loves me and how sorry she is to have lost her patience with me. I know this at the time because it's what always happens when she yells at me. She doesn't usually yell at me like this, but whenever she does, it's followed by a) tears, b) hugs, c) "sweet boy," and d) apology. It's a predictable pattern, so I don't really mind it that much.

"Mother—" A few years ago, I started calling her Mother instead of Mom because of the John Lennon song "Mother," which is a better song than the Genesis song "Mama." I do not know of any songs called "Mom," though there is "Stacy's Mom," but that doesn't count. "I ran into this bathroom by mistake after spilling an energy drink while you were talking to Dr. Sloane, and I mopped it up with paper towels as best I could, but I thought I should use the hand dryer before I go outside with a wet crotch. See?"

"Do you have to call me *Mother*?" she asks. "You make me feel like I'm eighty years old." Mother's age is a sensitive subject to her. She says she feels like a nineteen-year-old trapped in a forty-two-year-old's body. Once I told her that she's aging better than Debbie Harry or Exene Cervenka. This made her cry.

"But . . ."

"I know, Hank, I know. John Lennon."

"Right!" I say, smiling. We've found some common ground at last.

"Do you get that the song is about his mother abandoning him? That's why he's screaming." She opens a stall door.

"Yes, he and Yoko were involved in primal scream therapy with Dr.—"

"Hank. I'm just saying that . . . Oh never mind. Get the

hell out of the ladies' room, will you? I have to pee." She's now perched above the toilet, slowly closing the door.

"But my pants—"

"Go! You haven't been in the room while I'm peeing since you were three. Out."

"Okay. I'll see you back in Chase's room."

"Great." She closes the door, and it makes a loud clack as she slams the lock into place.

I walk out of the women's bathroom. It crosses my mind to go into the men's room and try again with the hand dryer there, but given how Mother reacted to the whole scene, I figure it's best to just let it go.

Maybe this isn't the best idea, though. When I get back to Chase's room, the first thing he does is point at me and laugh. "Dude, you look like you blew a load!"

"Great. Thank you."

"Hey, at least you tried something new, right?"

"Yeah."

"It's good for you. I'm looking out for you. You gotta break out of your routine."

"By drinking disgusting beverages and spilling them on myself?"

"It's not about the drink. It's about your attitude. You know? It's about not getting set in your ways like you're an old man or something."

"I'm not set in my ways! Last week I bought a Buffalo Springfield album! Due to my dislike of Stephen Stills, I vowed I would never buy that band's work, but then I heard 'Mr. Soul' and—"

Chase looks at the door, then whispers, "Nursing student. Play along." When I walked in, Chase was sitting up straight in bed. He was not kissing his substantial biceps. He only does that in front of the mirror at home. But he was sitting up straight. Now he slumps down and runs a hand through his long blond hair, messing it up when it looked perfect before.

A young woman with long, honey-blond hair, too much makeup, and very large breasts comes into the room. "Hi, I'm Patti," she says.

"With an 'i' like Patti Smith with an 'i,'" or with a 'y' like Patty Smyth with a 'y'?" I say, curious. Chase glares at me.

Patty—or should I say Patti—raises her blue-shadowed eyelids, looks at me, says, "With an 'i,'" and turns to Chase.

"So I'm studying nursing here, and I just need to take your vitals, if that's okay," Patti says.

"All . . . right," Chase croaks out.

"You had your knee scoped, is that right?" Patti asks.

"Yeah. Listen, you haven't heard anything about my prognosis, have you? It's just that I play lacrosse, and our team has a real shot at the NCAA title this year. But it's not the lax, you know, it's the scholarship. If I can't play, I can't pay, and then . . . I don't know. I guess I'll be pulling espresso shots instead of going to college. It's just . . . I feel like my whole future's on the line here, you know?"

Parts of what he says are true. He does go to college on a scholarship to play lacrosse. His team, however, has never in the history of the school been ranked higher than number twenty-seven nationally. And if he lost his scholarship, he could fall back on the substantial college savings Dad's parents put away. Of course I don't point any of this out. I do not contradict Chase when he talks to a girl any more than I try to run onto the field when he plays lacrosse; I know much more about music than he does, but there are certain areas where I defer to his expertise.

"Wow," Patti says, pumping his blood pressure cuff, "you must be really worried."

"Yeah." Chase nods. "I guess I am."

"Well, I'll tell you what. I'm gonna go ask around and see what I can find out, and I'll check back here and let you know what I hear, okay?"

"Thank you," Chase says. "You're really kind. You're already a better nurse than anybody else I've seen here."

Patti blushes, smiles, mouths the words "Thank you" at Chase, and leaves the room. As soon as he's sure she is gone, Chase turns to me and whispers, "Watch and learn, my boy! Watch and learn!"

I have the watching down, but I really don't feel like I've learned anything. Having a girl talk to me, smile at me like that, like me, want to kiss me—that seems as impossible as Johnny, Joey, and Dee Dee Ramone rising from the grave for a Ramones reunion tour. Impossible, but wouldn't it be cool if it actually happened?

CHAPTER 3
LIANA

Away from the hollow echoes of the bathroom and back in the creepy quiet of the hospital corridor, I walk toward room 202. The linoleum floor is speckled white, with the odd dark blue and aqua tiles thrown in for some reason. Cheer, I suppose, even though, let's get real, people, it's a hospital, and the only reason you're here is because of bad things. Hospitals are like black holes—which sound like harmless pits a kid could dig with a shovel, but they're not; they're theoretical regions in space, but theoretical or not, their gravitational pull is so strong there's nothing—no human, Mack truck, tank, not even light itself—that can escape its clutches. Hospitals suck you in too, only you don't have the free-floating escape of space. You just have linoleum. With one foot on blue and the other on white, like some demented version of Twister. I wonder if there are scenarios that are happy in hospitals. Diseased foot? Nope. Tragic accident? No again. Stitches? Even minor injuries aren't reason to smile.

I get almost all the way to 202 before I remember the note. I leave it where it is and look toward the room. The door is open enough that I can see in a little. Not all the way but enough to see their feet. My dad's bony ones are hunked on top of the meshy white blanket; my mother's, clad in flats that are too confining for this time of year, are near the foot of the bed. God forbid she wears a sandal. Flip-flops would signal total anarchy. I cough, giving them fair warning that I'm coming in, just in case they're talking about anything significant, which I highly doubt.

The feet shift. I thumb my tattoo.

"Liana!" Dad's voice is overly enthusiastic, the kind of happy you get at an airport, not a hospital.

I scrape my feet along the floor and go into the room, and suddenly I find one reason you could be happy here. On the television, the one that's pinned to the corner of the ceiling at an improbably awkward angle, is the hospital network channel. Sometimes they show rehab info, like what it'll be like if you broke your hip and are going home. Other times they provide all this info on sodium and dietary restrictions if you have diabetes or something. For the past hours that we've been camped out here, I've seen a lot of this. But not what's playing now.

My mother opens her mouth to speak but is captivated by the shot on the screen: a newborn, wrapped in a blue-and-pink-trimmed blanket, a tiny white hat perched on its head. A baby, I think, realizing that I would sound stupid saying it. That's a reason to be happy at a hospital. Having a baby. "Bringing a newborn home is the happiest day of your life. But it's also a time of great change." The voice is scratchy, coming out of the remote that's looped over my father's guardrail. I look at my parents and watch my father fumble with the remote to change the station or switch it off. I take a last glance at the impossibly small person on the screen. Giving birth would be the only good reason, a happy reason, to be at a hospital. Happy for most.

"I thought you were getting food?" My mother's tight bun has started to fray, giving her the appearance of having rubbed a balloon on her head. Static. "You know how you get if you wait too long. I should have brought something from home. The bran muffins from this morning." She gives me a withered look, asking me wordlessly not to be another person demanding her care.

"I'm fine." I shrug her off.

My dad motions for me to join him on the bed, and I perch on the edge, realizing to my annoyance that no, I didn't get anything to eat, and yes, I am nearing that semi-woozy stage where I feel half here and half somewhere else. Then again, I feel that not only when I'm hungry. I flash for a second to kissing Jett Alterman under the bleachers. If only it hadn't been during a heat wave, it would have been perfect. Or nearly perfect, except for the marching band's practice that made my head ring with cymbals, and the fact that Marissa Michaels and her wastoid crew kept giggling from under the neighboring set of bleachers. Was I semi there then, too? Jett turned out to be so much less than the emotionally in-tune lead singer he promised to be. Or at least that I thought he was. Turns out he didn't even want to sing. He'd just stumbled into it. And stumbled into me too. That's the thing about kisses: they're supposed to be magic, like the physics of two separate beings with their own splitting cells and genetic codes somehow finding each other and then, despite gravity's pull yanking them elsewhere, their mouths meet. But when it's just a coincidence—stumbling—how can that be it? That's just objects bumping, colliding in the universe for no good reason. The note in my pocket chafes at my thigh skin. I frown. Maybe it's not just hunger bothering me. But hunger makes it worse.

"She needs food," my mother says to my dad, as though I'm an inanimate object. Or, an inanimate object if it actually consumed food.

"I'm due for a meal myself." Dad tugs at his call button, summoning a nurse who will no doubt produce a smile and a tray of watery potatoes, floppy toast, and perhaps—if he's lucky—red Jell-O.

"Going for the ultra-spicy tonight, huh?" I raise my eyebrows and flip my hair out of my face. The room is so bright. It'll be a relief to leave here and settle into a routine at the science lab: the dim air, the dull sound of the air conditioner, it's easier than the stark reality of this place.

"Very funny. You know I can't wait to get out of here." Dad's face shows his worry, though. He will talk about craving Mexican food or maybe curry, but the truth is that he's concerned.

"Any news?" I pick at the hem of my shirt. The boy in the bathroom knew Squeeze. Or at least he sounded like he did. Then again, guys do that sometimes—say they like what you like, or know what you know, just to get closer to you. I should know, because I do this too. Say if there's a guy I want to kiss and I haven't—I could study him, find out what he likes; it's so easy, really, to spew sports facts or make up some passion for theater even though I only like musicals, which I keep fairly hidden because, really, what's a science-oriented person like me, one whose main loves are space and kissing, doing liking musicals? Anyway, maybe Bathroom Boy does know Squeeze. Maybe he's moody enough to like Tom Waits, but fun-loving enough to charge into the wrong bathroom and like Squeeze. I crack up now, thinking about the whole bathroom scene. Talk about objects colliding in space.

"What?" My mother grins back, wanting to know, always to know, what I'm thinking and yet rarely telling me her thought bubbles. "What? What's so funny?" She looks hopeful that I'll spill, but I just shake my head.

"Just thinking something funny," I tell her, and laugh.

"Redundant," Dad announces. He's not being mean, just his usual grammar-devil self. He designed that computer program, the one everyone uses to make sure they're not spelling everything wrong, and even though his days are jammed more with flights and meetings now, he still nitpicks the words I use.

"You know what?" I pat my dad's leg as though it doesn't belong to him. And really, when you see someone in the hospital, in the sterile sheets and embarrassingly thin gown, it feels like that. Like everything is disconnected from everything else. "I'm starving."

I stand up and head for the door—again. My mother checks her watch. "He said we'd hear back by now. Don't you think it's late? They should have the results by now."

My dad pushes the call button again. Now he can ask for a meal tray *and* if he's going to live. Which of course we all know he is—because this is what always happens. To him.

"Want anything?" I ask them.

Mom considers for a minute. "Pretzels?" Leave it to her to pick the blandest thing the vending machine has to offer. "Unsalted."

"Dad?" I stare at him. He's very tall, so seeing him lying down is strange. No matter how many times we wind up back here, there's a part of me that finds it disorienting, the way that scientists describe the re-entry to Earth after being in space. It's not the weightlessness that bothers them, it's coming back to gravity. I hold my own hands, thumbing my palm the way this guy Julian Nichols did when we made out backstage after his play last year. He was a big musical theater guy. His lips were a little dry, but not so dry that they were chapped. I imagined him going on to star on Broadway, maybe in London's West End, giving me a signal from the stage to show he was thinking of me, as though any high school kisses matter. He held my face when he kissed me, which I liked, even though I figured he'd practiced the move. It felt dramatic and he was heading to NYU for film school in the fall, so it made sense. So did the fact that he later hooked up with the girl who played Sarah Brown to his Sky Masterson in the production of *Guys and Dolls*. "Dad?"

Dad fiddles with his IV line. "This damn tape is making me itchy." My mother tries to help him. "And no, no food for me. Better stick to the prescribed diet."

It doesn't take a shrink to make a connection between my dad's major hypochondria and my rather ruthless love of kissing. Then again, my mother is kind of a shrink and she's never said anything. Then again, she doesn't know the extent of my potential slutdom because, as far as she's concerned, I've been kissed exactly twice—once when she saw a boy in seventh grade peck me on the cheek, which doesn't count, and once when she interrupted the basement kiss at my house. That counted. I was pressed up against the wall, staring into Jonah Jacobs's eyes, mesmerized by his mouth. We'd bonded over Bob Dylan, who we both loved, over calculus, at which he excelled, and Uranus, not my favorite planet, but funny in a totally juvenile way. "Hey, Uranus," he'd called me, and I'd laughed because my last name is Planet. "It's pronounced *pluh-net*," I'd said, and looked to the side like Joni Mitchell on the cover of *Blue*. I'm a master of looking like I'm somewhere else. He'd stared at me a while, and I'd thought, just for a few minutes, that we could wind up together. Like not basement together, but together—seamed.

"Here she comes." My mother points to the doorway, where a fresh-faced nurse brings my dad's chart. She studies it and remains unfazed. This is probably because, even though I am not a doctor, I think there's not much to be fazed by in there. Around three times a year my dad has these freak-outs. Attacks, you might call them, although he doesn't. Once he was flying from Austin back home from some conference, and he got left-arm pain. Then chest pain. But it wasn't a coronary. Once he'd been home for only four hours, like a layover at our house between travels, and started dry heaving. With neck pain. But it wasn't meningitis as he feared. Each time, he comes here, gets admitted "for observation," and winds up going home the next day. It's part annoying, part tedious, and just the smallest bit scary because I guess there's always that possibility of *what if*.

On Earth, we can see back in time until a point about 100,000 years after the big bang. But my parents can't see back even four months ago when Dad was right where he is now, clad in a gown and poked with an IV for no good reason except his own nerves. I touch the metal of the doorjamb as I brush past the nurse and head for vending-machine bliss. I can hear her relaying the blood-work results to my dad. I don't know what it all means, but he's taking the news well.

"Oh, great! Whoa." He sighs as I exit. "So, no more tests? What about sed rate or specific gravity?" He knows all the terms now. His voice is at once relieved and sad. He enjoys not being poked and prodded, but maybe having the investigation. Having someone spend the time, I guess, looking into what is going on unseen in his cells, his plasma, his organs.

I mouth the words *specific gravity*. Good band name. I check my mother's face. She is furrowed on the brow but already starting to pack it in—looking around the room at what needs to be packed up, what needs to be dealt with at home.

My father will be back on his feet tonight, tomorrow morning, latest, and back to jetting all over the globe in no time. My mother will drive him to the airport, which she only ever does after one of these fits, and then we'll be back to normal until the next one, which—if past experience means anything, which of course it does—will be around the end of August.

I put my fingers on my mouth, feeling the puff of my lower lip, wondering if anyone I've ever kissed longs for me. Longs for me the way I long for another new kiss, something I don't yet know. Like I said, there's some connection between those medical tests my dad desires and my own lip frenzy, but I'm not a shrink and my mother's not really one either.

"I want candy," I say, and then, remembering that those words also form lyrics, I sing them. My fingers rest on the vending-machine glass until I think of all the sad, sick people who have touched the same glass, and I shove my hands deep into my jeans. The paper in my right-hand pocket scratches at my palm, but I ignore it, wishing I'd worn shorts. I'll be too hot when I get outside, but I dressed for the science lab, where I will live all summer, and it's always freezing in there.

Peanut M&M's. Wafer cookies. Blue tortilla chips. Fritos. Salty or sweet? My whole body leans into the machine. How many snacks are contained here? Six rows across, eight rows down, forty-eight possibilities of snack food, and only one will be the perfect fit for what I crave now. Krinkle Cheezies? I shake my head. Cheese balls. Tiny planets of horrifically bright orange. Swedish fish. What makes them Swedish? I suddenly really want to know, but there's no one to ask. Not even Cat, my best friend, who is blessed with a cool name and an even cooler summer job for which she left school a whole three days early—testing gelato flavors in Italy because her mother imports the stuff. So she's not here for a candy consult or anything else. And there aren't many people I could just call and ask such a weird question.

"E6," I decide in a whisper and sling in an obnoxious amount of change and wait for my snack.

"Plain M&M's," comes the voice. "A bold choice."

I check over my shoulder. Intense and inky. Dark and daring. The boy from the bathroom. "Bathroom Boy," I say to him. His pants are dry at least. He reaches down and collects my snack, tearing into them without asking, and chewing too loudly on a handful of my own personal would-be stash of candies.

"Bathroom Boy," he says, and considers it. "I've been called worse."

CHAPTER 4
HANK

Chase kicks me out of the room when Patti comes back. This is so he can "work his magic" on her to "get her digits." I suppose Chase is arrogant when he says he is working his magic, but it feels appropriate. Getting girls to like you enough to give you their phone numbers, to kiss you, to do whatever else goes on behind the door of Chase's room, whatever goes on in his dorm room, is so impossible for me that it might as well be magic.

Not that I'm not getting better. The bullying stopped early in ninth grade, and with Allie's help I'm usually able to have a rudimentary conversation that appears normal, as long as I stay focused. But once you make a reputation, everything you do is seen through that lens. My position outside the social mainstream was cemented early in the ninth grade, and I don't even understand how one moves into the part of the social landscape where girls look for their potential boyfriends. I suppose it's fair to say I don't really understand the social landscape at all. I blunder around in it, lacking the map that most people take for granted.

I live in a beach town, and summertime is particularly painful in this respect. The town is awash in bikini-clad beauties, and the few not already dating my brother appear to have written off our entire family.

I'm thinking about this as I wander down the hall to the vending machines. I have never met or corresponded with any members of The Mooney Suzuki, a garage rock revival band, but when they mapped the brain of a young man as having a little room for music and the rest for girls, they might have been describing me. Though I guess I have more room for music than most people.

And then the girl with the breasts is there at the vending machines, and she calls me Bathroom Boy. She smiles, so I don't think she's being cruel. But I'm not sure. Even still, me in the wrong bathroom, suspicious stain on my crotch and everything, this girl was kind to me, and that simply doesn't happen to me very often.

So when I see her again, that little voice I usually hear as Allie's, which gives me tips to remember in conversation, goes away, and I just start eating M&M's.

"You know," I tell the girl with the breasts, "Van Halen had a provision in their tour contract where they had to have a bowl of M&M's backstage with all the brown ones sorted out." I pop a brown M&M into my mouth. "But I can never tell the difference. Can you? I mean, they used to say the green ones make you horny, but I've never found that to be the case, and if I had my eyes closed, I would certainly never be able to tell you what color I'm eating. Like this." I close my eyes, reach into the bag, and pop an M&M into my mouth. "I have no idea. Blue? Orange? Did you see what it was?"

"No," she says.

I stick my tongue out and observe the half-dissolved candy shell. "Well, it's mostly white now, but I guess it still proves my point. So my question is, why did Van Halen object? I mean, what's the difference?"

"At least they got to eat *their* M&M's," the girl says, her dark eyebrows raised up and her arms crossed over her chest.

I look at my hand, and I'm suddenly embarrassed. "I'm eating your candy," I say.

"Yep."

"I'm sorry. I came here to get some M&M's because Patti came back and Chase told me to scram, and I was so happy to see you that I forgot about the fact that I hadn't actually bought the M&M's."

The girl looks at me. I guess she's saying something to me with her expression. I don't know what it is. Now I'm nervous. I've forgotten to listen, I've forgotten to take a moment to think about whether another person might want to hear what's going on in my brain, all the advice that helps me navigate the world.

"Let me just buy you some," I say. I feed the machine a dollar, press E6, and the rack circles so a pack of M&M's

moves halfway out of the row and doesn't fall. "Crap. Wait, I have some more change. Then we'll have an extra bag. I wonder if they had the M&M thing with Sammy Hagar, or if that was just a David Lee Roth thing. Sammy Hagar recently sold his tequila brand to Seagram's. So I guess he's still making money even if he's not in the reconstituted Van Halen." I feed the machine, and this time two bags pop out. I dig them out and hand them to . . . the girl.

"Hey," I say. "Do you have a name besides The Girl in the Squeeze Shirt? Squeeze was going to reunite too—they did it for that VH1 show, but Jools Holland wasn't interested. Maybe they could have gotten Paul Carrack, though. I think they should have done it." I suddenly remember that I'm supposed to pause from time to time and check in with my interlocutor. "What do you think?"

"Uh, I think sometimes it's better to know when to stop," she says. She touches her lips with her fingers.

"I guess so. I mean, look at The Who, if you can still call them that. Pete Townshend says the band was never the same after Keith Moon died, which I guess everybody knew, but—"

"Well, listen, I gotta go. You want the extra pack of candy? You bought them, after all." She moves away from the candy machine. I do not say Please don't walk away, I promise I will shut up if you'll just stay here, girls never talk to me, even at work I only talk to the male customers, or they anyway are the only ones who talk to me. I am thinking all of these things, but people get disconcerted when you say exactly what's on your mind.

"No, they're a present for you. For your trouble."

She stops and smiles at me. "What trouble?"

"Well, I forgot to . . . because I ate your M&M's."

She gives me another look. I really wish I understood it. If you can't read, you can walk through town and not understand the DO NOT ENTER signs or know what any of the stores are, so you'll go the wrong way down the street and ask if you can drop off your dry cleaning at a dentist's office. I guess my life is like this. That's what Allie tells me. She is female but doesn't count because she's a social worker and our relationship is strictly professional.

This is what she told me when I asked her if she wanted to go to a movie. She very nicely talked to me about how that would be inappropriate, and if I would work on the things she teaches me, I could meet other girls, girls my own age, to go to the movies with.

The funny thing is that I didn't have a crush on Allie. I just knew that she liked old movies and *High School Confidential* was playing at the Wilson Square Theatre. Little Richard, Eddie Cochran, Fats Domino, Gene Vincent, and The Platters all perform in that movie.

Allie tells me there are signs everywhere in the way people act, in the tone of their voice, in the way they hold their head, and I can't read the signs. So sometimes I go speeding down the road in the wrong direction. I'm afraid I may have just done this by giving this girl the extra M&M's, even though it just seemed to be the right thing to do.

"That's sweet," she says finally. "I'm Liana, by the way. What are you in for?"

"What?"

"In the hospital. Why are you eating M&M's here instead of in a less heinous place?" She picks at something on her shirt right where the Z is.

"Oh, my brother, he's got some kind of lacrosse injury and—"

"Do you have a name?"

"Yeah. It's Hank."

"Hank? Really?"

"Well, my real name is Henry. I was named for Henry Rollins, you know, from Black Flag, and the Rollins Band, as well as various spoken word performances and now a weekly show on IFC. I saw Peaches on his show once. She frightened me."

"I don't know what you're talking about." Her hair is dark brown and long, with choppy shorter parts at the front. The kind of hair a librarian would have in an old school music video such as I watch on VH1 Classic from time to time, the kind of hair that starts tightly wound up to show the seriousness of the character, and then, once she unpins it or whatever, is transformed. Only Liana's already like that right now. Her hair is down, but not as huge as the hair of the girl in the video for Adam Ant's "Goody Two Shoes," but that video is from 1982, the year that Mother refers to as "The Biggest of the of Big Hair Years."

In between her hair and her breasts, there is her mouth. And when Liana smiles, as she's doing right now, she looks twinkly.

I do not tell her that she looks like a girl from an '80s video.

31

I have learned that people don't always like these comparisons. Though Chase quite enjoys hearing that he has Henry Rollins's body, Kurt Cobain's hair, and Justin Timberlake's face. Which I intended as a put-down.

"Ah. I'm sorry you don't know what I'm talking about. I have that problem." I take a breath and slow down. "Anyway, when I was nine, I discovered Hank Williams, who, while he is a country artist, is kind of a godfather of rock and roll. George Thorogood covered "Move It on Over." Most people don't even know that's a Hank Williams song. Though technically it's an old R & B—"

"Yeah. I certainly never knew that. Well, Hank, it was nice meeting you, and I've got to—"

"I work at Planet Guitar. If you ever want me to help you with a guitar or something, you should stop by. I also know a lot about our selection of guitar effects, so if you ever need help with a wah-wah pedal or your fuzzbox, I could help you. I can give you my employee discount."

She's laughing and twinkling. I wasn't aware I'd made a joke. "Did you just offer to help me with my fuzzbox?"

"Well, if you play guitar. Or bass. Captain Beefheart covered 'Diddy Wah Diddy' with so much fuzzbox on the bass that—"

"I'll remember that," she says, but she's smiling and something doesn't match up between how she's looking at me and what she's saying. She's about to leave again.

"Listen, Liana, you're a girl, right?"

She keeps cocking her head at me and smiling. "That's why I was in the women's bathroom."

"So can I ask you something about my brother?"

"Uh. Okay."

"He's what's referred to as a ladies' man. And normally he gets the girls by being a big Carville University lacrosse-playing jock guy, and I always thought they were responding to the strength and confidence he projects."

"Sounds like a good theory."

"But then Patti, this student nurse, came in, and he acted all weak and scared. And she came back in just two minutes, and I had to leave the room."

Liana smiles. "Ah."

"What?"

"He's reading the situation. Why do you think girls study nursing?"

I remember to glance over at the vending machines because Allie told me people find it disconcerting if you look right at them all the time even if you are supposed to be paying attention to them. "Because they're interested in science?"

"No. That's why girls study *medicine*. Girls study nursing because they like taking care of people. So here's your brother playing 'I'm a big strong athlete but I need you to take care of me.' It's a genius move." She nods her head and flashes that smile again.

People say things like this a lot. They talk about moves and strategies when they're just talking about how to talk to each other. I can't even imagine how that works. Which is why I am just saying what's on my mind. I wonder what kind of move that is.

"I don't know . . . It just doesn't make any sense to me. You know? Music makes sense to me."

"You just have to figure out what the other person is interested in, what they want, and try to be that for them." She stops talking briefly and looks at the ceiling. I look up there as well but don't see what she sees, so I take the opportunity to look at her breasts again. Girls don't like it when you stare at their breasts, even if, like Liana, they have really tight shirts on. Allie did not tell me this. Chase did. Liana looks back at me, and I snap my eyes up to her face. "Does your brother like science?"

I laugh. Chase scrapes by in school on his lacrosse-playing ability and an inexplicable fondness for history. I don't think he's ever broken a C in a science class. "Not at all."

"Well, I do. Let's go meet him, and I'll reveal my love of planetary science, and I'll bet you he suddenly develops an interest in astronomy."

"I'll be surprised if Chase can even feign interest in things that don't revolve around him."

Liana laughs.

There are certain lines in songs that I can make out but fundamentally don't understand. Like when someone says "my heart just flipped" or "my heart skipped a beat," or when Buddy Holly asks his heartbeat why it stops when his baby kisses him. I should say I never understood those lines until I heard Liana laugh at my joke about Chase.

I've certainly heard laughter from girls before, but normally it's the behind-the-hand laughter one might refer to as sniggering. Liana's laughter was not like that. It seemed to stop my heart for just a moment.

"Let's go!" She reaches back and pulls at my arm. Her hand on my arm feels like an electric shock. But in a good way. I stand still for a moment, thinking about The Doors' "Touch Me," but I can't really say, like Jim Morrison does, *I am not afraid*, because I am afraid, though I can't really say of what.

Liana tugs on my arm and suddenly we're walking down the hall. "Liana!" some lady I assume is her mom calls from down the hall. "Will you come here for a minute?"

"I'll be right there," she calls, but then to me says, "Which room?"

"Right up here on the left."

"Great. You can say we're classmates who just bumped into each other. Where do you go to school?"

"Melville West," I tell her.

"Oh. I go to East, but they're both big schools." She shrugs and her T-shirt rises just a little, riding up to reveal a little piece of her lower back. I check for a tattoo at the base of her spine and see none. Chase refers to tattoos in that spot as "tramp stamps" and has told me that I should always check for the tramp stamp, so I do, though I suppose it means different things to us. I assume that a girl with the tramp stamp would like Chase and is therefore inappropriate for me.

She smiles at me, and we walk into the room. Nurse Patti is gone. Mom still hasn't come back from the bathroom. I wonder if she fell in. That's what she always used to say to us when we took a long time in the bathroom. "Hey," I say to Chase.

"Hey Sq—Hank, my man!" Chase says, smiling at Liana. He flicks his hand through his hair and shifts to the side so his bandaged leg is fully visible from where we're standing. "Who's your friend?"

"This, uh, this is Liana. We have science class together."

"I had to hide from my mom," Liana says. "And when Hank told me you went to Carville, I had to ask—Oh, how's the knee by the way?"

"Piece of cake," Chase says. His eyes roam over her. His expression is one I can't identify.

"Anyway," Liana continues, looking at Chase, "I'm starting to think about college, you know. I'm applying this fall . . . and I know Carville has a fantastic observatory. I'm just wondering if you know anything about the astronomy program or the—"

"It's an awesome facility. It's really—I mean, for me it's a thrill just to be able to see Dr. Borneaz on campus. You know? I'm like, here's this guy who's a giant in his field, and there he is eating a breakfast burrito two tables away from me."

"Wow," Liana says. I know from her plan that she is faking her surprise or enthusiasm. I can't help staring at Chase. I would be surprised if he could name all nine planets, or eight now since Pluto got demoted.

"You should definitely visit. On a clear night you can see Uranus."

Liana laughs. "Well, listen, I've gotta go. Come on,

Hank, you promised you'd buy me a cup of coffee."

"No, I bought you the M&M's, remembe— Ow!" She stomps on my foot. And I still don't get it.

Chase says, "Hank. Come here for a minute."

I lean over his bed, and he whispers in my ear, "She wants you to go with her. Don't be an idiot! Go, stud!"

"Oh. Thank you!" I say.

"Just looking out for you," Chase says to me, but smiles at Liana.

"Okay," I say to her. "Let's get you that cup of coffee." We begin walking out of the room as Mother comes bustling back in.

"Oh. Hello!" Mother says.

"Hi, Mother," I say.

Mother rolls her eyes and sighs. "Most people call me Helen," Mother says to Liana. "Hank, introduce me to your friend."

"Oh, sorry. Mother, this is Liana. We go to school together." Mother smiles and stares. It looks like tears are beginning to form in her eyes. "And we have to go get coffee."

"Nice to meet you," Liana says, and this time I'm the one who's pulling her out of the room.

CHAPTER 5
LIANA

"So there's the universe, right?" I sip my iced coffee and chew on the straw, looking not just at Hank but at all the people scattered around us in the hospital cafeteria.

Hank nods. "And there's Universal Records, which at one point was the—"

"Hank?" I've known the guy all of an hour—if you count the bathroom as the first point of knowing—and already I can tell he's about to spew info about music. But not really about songs, exactly. More like background details. I imagine he's got buckets of CDs at home, an iPod full of songs he can expose me to.

"Oh." He fiddles with the wooden stirrer, making it into a mini guitar. "Was I about to barge in on your part of the conversation?"

I nod and check my watch. "I have to go but . . . I was

talking about my project?" I shrug. Soon enough I'll be submerged in the lab, lulled by the whir of A.C. and meticulous note-taking. Notes. Not the kind of notes you randomly shove into someone's locker, which make them wonder about their place in the universe. More the kind you hand in for extra credit. "I'm not exactly sure what the report will end up being. For now I'm more like scratching the surface."

"Of space?" Hank continues to strum the lilliputian guitar, doing chords and everything.

"Are you playing a real song?" I point to his fretwork. I attempted, for all of four classes, to play the guitar, but gave up. Maybe I didn't even want to play. I love music, but at the time I mainly was following this guy Simon, who played acoustic funk at Espresso Love, this coffee place on Ocean Boulevard in our thriving metropolis of downtown Melville. Espresso Love was the highlight of knowing Simon. Turns out people who play funk aren't necessarily funky.

Hank looks up from his guitar and makes eye contact with me for the first time. "It's 'Satellite of Love'—Lou Reed. It just seemed appropriate—you know, because of your project."

"I don't know that song," I tell him. He looks truly surprised. No one else in the cafeteria seems to notice we are two virtual strangers having coffee on the last day of school. Or the first day of summer vacation, depending on how you look at it. One of the basic tools I learned way back in Earth Science was the art of predicting. Predictions are crucial for experiments in the lab, but in life they don't always make sense. For example: how the hell would I be able to predict meeting Hank?

"It's a good song. Not really great, but twangy and, not that I know you or anything, but you'd probably like it. If you like Squeeze, which you probably do because you're wearing . . ." His voice trails off, and we both look at my shirt. Or maybe I look at my shirt and he checks out what's under my shirt. But I don't care. Because of the note. Because I know I disagree with what the note says. And because we're in a hospital and because Hank isn't like a regular person. Or maybe I just think he's not like the people I normally hang out with. He's more pensive. Or more something. "Do you want to hear it sometime?"

I shrug and look in his eyes. "Yeah." They're really light green. Sea-glass color. "So I was telling you about the explosions. In the universe. One's short—like only several seconds. And the other's even shorter—maybe just a fraction of a second." I take my straw out of the plastic cup and flick coffee on my shirt by accident, then try and wipe it off with my hand. "Anyway, astronomers had no idea where the bursts came from. And you have to know the source . . ."

One table over, an old man suddenly starts sobbing. He's just sitting there crying, in front of the nurses with their frozen yogurts and the doctors in their water-blue scrubs and the various visitors like us. My stomach churns. He's so sad. Maybe his wife is sick. Or he is. Or something else I can't guess. I look at Hank. He doesn't seem to notice.

"Liana? Explosions?" Hank nudges me with a flick of his fake guitar.

This spring I got the idea for a project that would basically try to make sense of why stars twinkle, which sounds

40

too dumb to say, but sounds a bit better when I think about the other issues, the explosions, the unknowns in space. Or things we think we know. So my job is to study refracting light and stars and shifts in moon phases and try to write about it in a coherent way, which is harder than it sounded in my mind when I first came up with the idea. I sigh and try to explain to Hank. "Right. Explosions. Now this famous scientist has shown that the explosions—short-duration bursts they call them—are caused by collisions of two really dense objects. Like neutron stars or a black hole or something."

"Sounds complicated."

"It is." I collect my coffee debris; straw and sugar packet wrapper. "This coffee sucks." Hank nods.

"Espresso Love's is way better. They play decent music, and on Thursdays, or if it's really slow, I'm sometimes able to DJ there."

He likes Espresso Love. More points in his favor. "With records and everything?"

Hank blushes as though I caught him lying. "No. Not like that. I just meant . . . I have a solid two weeks' worth of music on my hard drive, plus another probably week and a half on an external hard drive. And I'll burn things and bring them there and play whatever I want—like a soundtrack." He stands up, following me to the trash can to chuck out his own coffee, which wasn't iced because it turns out even though it's summer, he doesn't like ice in any of his drinks. He asked if I thought that was weird, but I told him I didn't because of my own root beer issues, and he was more than happy to hear about how I only really like soda from a glass bottle. One thing that's nice about meeting someone random like this, I guess, is that you can just say stuff like that and not care how it sounds.

"So you can control the atmosphere," I say as we slide through the corridor past the pathetic gift shop with its newborn outfits in pink and blue, the overdyed carnations, the get-well cards, and junky books sold to help people pass the time. "Like the moon pulls the tides."

"Yeah, I guess. I never thought of it that way."

"How *did* you think about it?" I ask him when we're near room 202. My parents are probably analyzing every bit of information from the doctors, obsessing over cholesterol numbers and the like. "Because that's how I would. You get to choose the songs and make people feel a certain way while they're just sitting there, innocently ordering their lattes." I grin at him.

He shakes his head, his unkempt hair momentarily covering his eyes. His brother's hair is surfer blond, tousled, but in a very planned way. Hank's is less studied. Unstudied, in fact, and darker blond. The kind of hair that threatens to turn blond if you live on the beach, but not if you work at Planet Guitar. "I just play what I want. If I feel like hearing Big Audio Dynamite, then I'll play it. And if right after that I segue into an English Beat song, that's just because I can. Not because I'm, like, wanting to make the audience swoon." He cracks up with the last part, affecting an Elvis stance as he says it.

"But if you play, say, 'The End of the Party,' which is one of my favorite Beat songs, by the way, then it fills the room with a certain energy. Electrodes or currents or just . . ." I think of that song. Of hearing it in my own room and hearing it, too, in my head at a certain party this spring when I found out, finally, what it was like to kiss Pren Stevens, the lead singer.

"*'Say it now, you know there's never a next time,'*" Hank says, his voice monotone. We're paused directly in front of 202.

"Great line. Of course, then they contradict themselves later in the song by saying there's always a next time. But . . ." I falter, standing in my uncomfortable jeans, not because I want to get rid of Hank, but because I don't want to. Not for any reason I can pinpoint, but hanging with him beats having to deal with my parents before I get on with the rest of my summer.

My mother chooses this exact moment to stick her head out, ostrich-style, of the room. Her whole face yells perky even though her voice stays totally calm. "Daddy's fine," she tells me, and casts a glance over at Hank.

"My dad's fine," I tell Hank just so I'm not standing there saying nothing and feeling weird.

Hank nods and looks over his left shoulder toward the room where his brother is getting stitched or snapped into place.

Chase *is* fine, I think, though not in the health-related way. I recall his rather buff physique, his sly smile. Total player. I stick my hands in my pockets so I don't seem too jittery from the caffeine buzz. My fingers toy with the note. The entire note is only one word. When I think about it, this whole moment, the hospital corridor and Hank and my mother recede. It's like even though I'm not the sick one, I somehow have the diagnosis in my pocket.

One word. When I first looked at it near my locker, I actually flipped it over thinking that there'd be more to it. Like whoever'd sent it had more to say. Or wanted to elaborate.

Slut.

First I thought this was proof the sender lacked brain power. Was less than stellar in the creativity department. Now I think they might win the Most Succinct award. Slut. Slut. The word is any part of speech—noun, adjective, and hey, if you believe the rumors, a verb. She sluts around. Doing what, exactly? Use your imagination, folks.

"Honey?" My mother beckons me back into the room.

I rejoin the waking world here in the corridor, and erase thoughts of Hank's brother's hotness.

"So . . ." I turn to Hank, who pushes the sleeve of his T-shirt up and bobs in place, probably desperate to leave. I think about saying 'See you later,' but I probably won't, so I don't. "I guess . . ."

Hank takes no cue from me because right before he darts off, he says, "There *is* a next time, though, right? Like the song. So you don't have to say whatever it is you were going to say. 'Say Say Say'—terrible song. Definitely Paul McCartney sinking to new lows, even by Wings standards."

"Hank?" I rub my eyes, wired from the coffee, tired from the day. It's been fun having this random interaction, but now it's starting to feel like work. Or maybe he's easy and the rest of life is hard. I can't tell right now.

Hank stops jabbering—finally—but can't stop his eyes

44

from swiveling down and up, sort of like he's trying to follow a fly. "So you're going?" I nod and move toward my mother, who is watching but pretending not to. "I'll see you Thursday, then," he says. I raise my eyebrows to ask why, but he does me the favor of rambling on. "At Espresso Love."

"The soundtrack?" I cross my arms so I'm sort of hugging myself. What is my prediction here? That we will meet at Espresso Love. Have coffee and never speak again? That I won't even show up? That we will ride off into the proverbial smoggy sunset? That someone will see us together and assume that he's just one of the many, that I'm up to my usual tricks, whatever people think those are, and we'll lock lips and then nothing? I bite my top lip and listen to the blips and bleeps coming from my father's room. You cannot predict anything.

He nods. "The soundtrack session. You'll meet me, okay?" He pauses. "Hey—now that's a great title, isn't it? For an album. *The Soundtrack Sessions.*"

It is a good title, but I can't tell him now. Now is me turning away from Hank, who is leaving. Now is me going over and hugging my dad and having him cry—not hard like the old man in the cafeteria; just a few quiet tears.

"I'm so relieved," he says. My mother nods, patting his shoulder as he hugs me. The hospital gown is scratchy against my face.

What gets me is that they don't talk about the pattern. They don't acknowledge the fact that we were here four months ago with his potential appendicitis-or-is-it-liver-cancer scare. If I confronted my mother, she and I would end up like those

45

explosions in the universe, only not as short-acting. My mother behaves as though holding a grudge is an Olympic sport. She still hasn't gotten over the kissing-in-the-basement incident. Only, her reaction is to not react. To avoid confrontation and discussion altogether.

My dad holds my hands in his, relieved. "What a day, huh?"

Wake up, people! I want to yell. He's fine! He will always be fine! It's something else that's the problem. But I can't scream this. And I can't even point to what exactly the other thing is that is the problem. I have my suspicions, though.

On the day of the soundtrack sessions I'm in the lab. When I'm there I feel the way some people must feel in church. The whole cavernous room is filled with all this mystery. Why are we here? How did we get here? Why does sunlight matter? What happens to water when it vaporizes? It's sacred somehow. The cool concrete walls tower over me, a safe and calm room with rows of soapstone tables, small sinks, and industrial shelves filled with Bunsen burners, textbooks, and model solar systems.

I take notes, jotting them in my looping scrawl onto the pages of my speckled green-and-white notebook, while studying the picture in front of me. It's an artist's rendition of a black hole devouring a neutron star. Mr. Pitkin, a.k.a. resident science guru, has left a question for me in my notebook and I have to answer it, or at least try to. He wants me to combine a whole ton of data from published star census reports in the hopes that mine will fit in there somewhere.

That's where I get the academic credit. Stars and planets, those are my real interest. In his immaculate printing he has written: *Condensation theory says that the planets developed through coagulation of dust grains in a disk of gas and dust. Do you have evidence to support this?* This is some people's idea of hell, spending a perfectly decent summer day answering, "Asteroids and comets all hold clues from the original solar system formation. A lot are traceable right to the origin of the solar system." I pause. What else . . . I jot "Plausible tracers from the early solar system are C-type asteroids and carbonaceous meteoroids," because this will show him I actually paid attention to his tutorial over winter break despite the fact that I was hung up on yet another musician. "Characterization includes very high carbon content . . . something like 4.4–4.6 BILLION years old. This is determined from radioactive dating." I stop there. He probably wouldn't mind this, the minimum effort. But I add a bit more. "Since the solar system is posited to have condensed about 4.6 billion years ago, these objects hold the most direct clues to that origin— based on their age." That's the amazing thing about objects: they have a life of their own and tell more, sometimes without a voice, than people.

After I answer Mr. Pitkin's question, I lean on the cool counter and put back the beaker I used as a water glass. It's totally not allowed, but I figure the chances of the glass being contaminated with any truly horrific germs is slim. I take a final swig and put it on the drying rack next to the lab's pride and joy. There's an amazing telescope, a LIGO, a Laser Interferometer Gravitational-Wave Observatory, that I get to use sometimes. It can detect all sorts of crazy happenings in the universe: collisions, even collapsed stars. Collapsed Stars.

Now that's the name for a band. I can tell Hank when I see him. Not that I've been planning on it, necessarily, but it's Thursday and Espresso Love is on my way home, especially if I want to do my usual beach walk, which I do. With my dad not only out of the hospital but already back at work (read: on a plane to Memphis or Des Moines or Indianapolis) and my mother treading a solid path from the kitchen to her home office, staying out of the house seems like the best choice. Plus, my best friend, Cat, is accessible in thought only, and all things considered, I liked talking to Hank. It was a relief, kind of, to just talk with him and not wonder if—or when—we might get together.

I check my watch. It's almost three. I don't have set lab hours, but I feel like a solid six is enough to call it a day. I log my hours on my study chart so Mr. Pitkin will have proof I've been here—more proof than my notes, I mean— and clean up the bits of paper, chewed-on pen cap, droppers. You have to leave a lab better than you found it. Immaculate. Pristine. Otherwise the next time you go to do your work, some debris or random bit of fluid could get into your experiment and screw it up.

At Espresso Love, Hank's not anywhere I can see. I check the coveted window seats, where the coolest kids hang out during the school year, and the back section, which is basically my local homework spot, always crammed near exam time, and since I can't find him, I just go to the counter and order myself an iced latte. Then I remember Hank doesn't like iced drinks and switch my order so he can have some if he wants.

"Actually, cancel that," I tell the server, because this is not a date. And even if it was a date, I shouldn't neg my coffee order because of some guy. Or what some guy wants to drink. That's my problem. I take my wallet out to pay. It's not so much a wallet as it is a case. My dad went to a four-day conference in San Francisco and brought back a bag full of goodies. Hollywood starlets might get gift bags filled with trendy clothes and lotions, but computer geeky dads just get things like mouse pads in the shape of cheese, and magnets with company logos on them. I like the case, though. It's a white plastic rectangle, semi-see-through, and meant to hold business cards, which of course I don't have and don't want. But it holds my one credit card, my folded cash, and my driver's license quite well. I hand the server five dollars and wait for my change. When it comes, I drop the coins into the tip bucket—because I refuse to carry around pennies and dimes only to have them fall out during my beach walks—and put the dollar bill back in my non-wallet. It slides in right next to my license, right next to the folded-up slut note, which for some reason I still have; all my forms of identification.

I take my cold drink and sit by the window, waiting for Hank. I figure I'll give him ten minutes to show, and if he doesn't, I'll leave. I realize that this number of minutes is arbitrary—I mean, we never said when we'd meet. In fact, I never told him I would. He just said he wanted to. Not exactly ideal conditions under which to perform an experiment of new friendship, if that's what this is.

49

Out the window, a girl from school, Melissa Winkle, walks hand in hand with some boy. They are every bit the essence of summer, with their hands linked, their feet in flip-flops, their limbs already summer brown. I do not tan like that. Even if I spent my days on the beach instead of in a lab, I would not be crispy tan. I'd be burned. I could try tanning with sunblock, but again—it's a risky experiment. I'll pass on the skin cancer, thanks. I wouldn't mind the hand-holding boy, though.

By definition, an experiment is a test with controlled conditions. A test you make to demonstrate something you know or think you know. You examine the validity of a hypothesis, or determine the efficacy of something previously untried. Outside, the summer couple kisses, and I feel the familiar swell of longing in my chest. My fingers go to my lips.

I sip my drink and look at my wallet, its contents hazily visible. The note.

I should be the experiment. Is she a slut or isn't she? Who can know except for me, right? If I disregard whatever's happened in the past. If I forget the littered kisses or hook-ups or whatever you want to call them, and just start now, where does that leave me? Or rather, who does that make me? Summer stretches out before me—iced coffees, beach walks, sound sessions, and all. The conditions are variable, but the experiment is on. Is Liana Planet what the note says she is? No. Or yes. We will find out. I'm about to document in my mind the ways in which we might test this hypothesis, but the door swings open with a whistle, and in walks Hank, looking maybe better than I remembered.

CHAPTER 6
HANK

In the early evening of the same day he had surgery, Chase leaves the hospital with a pair of crutches and Nurse Patti's phone number. At home, Chase pops a prescription painkiller and falls asleep, and Mother gives me a hug, cries, calls me her sweet boy, and apologizes for yelling at me in the bathroom.

Chase is able to switch from the heavy stuff to ibuprofen after a day. He hands the prescription bottle to Mother and says, "Mom, could you flush these please?"

Mother takes the bottle from Chase's hand, examines it, and says, "I thought you'd take all these whether you needed them or not."

"Yeah well," Chase says, "I got tired of hearing about Jeff Tweedy and Elvis all the time." He jerks his head toward me.

Mother looks at me, her brows knitted. "Hank. Can't you give your brother a break?"

"I just think it's interesting that both Jeff Tweedy and Elvis were addicted to prescription medicine. And of course there's a great deal of speculation that my namesake—"

"Okay, Rollins wasn't exactly straight edge, but I don't think he—"

"Died of a combination of painkillers and alcohol," I interject. "He suffered tremendous back pain, you know."

Mother closes her eyes, takes two deep breaths, and speaks to me in a very quiet voice. Chase hops out of the room, grinning.

"Henry. You are not named after Hank Williams. And he may well have suffered from back pain, but Chase was prescribed this medicine by a real doctor—not some Doctor Nick pill pusher—while he recovers from surgery. It's just— do you understand, does any part of you understand that when someone is in pain and taking medication that they might not enjoy hearing about people who died from taking medication? Does that make sense to you?" Mother's hands are on her hips, and her face is turning red.

"But, Mother, given the quantities of alcohol that Chase normally ingests, I just felt that he should be aware of the consequences of mixing prescription pain medicine with booze."

"You know what?" Mother barks. She doesn't finish her sentence. She closes her eyes and breathes, and finally speaks again, but quietly this time. "I guess you're right about that. I've talked to Chase about his drinking, but maybe your method will be more effective than my nagging."

After this, life returns pretty much to normal around our house. When Chase is not out with a girl, he is either working his upper body with weights in the basement or talking to or texting a girl.

Chase doesn't have to work. His lacrosse scholarship covers his tuition, and the fund Dad's parents established for his education expenses supplies what he refers to as "the other essentials" of college life. I understand that this means beer.

Mother works a great deal, picking up overtime whenever she can, which is often.

I go to work and sell guitars. I cannot touch my college money until I am actually in college, and even with my employee discount, the things I need are expensive.

Like, for example, the beautiful surf-green vintage Fender Jazzmaster that recently came into the shop. I could buy a very nice used car for the price of this guitar, but it's impossible to play a note-perfect version of The Ventures' "Walk Don't Run," or any surf instrumental at all, for that matter, on a car, especially the '94 Golf that is for sale down the street and which costs only slightly more than the Jazzmaster.

The Jazzmaster is out of reach.

Also out of reach, perhaps, is Liana. And yet she essentially agreed to meet me at Espresso Love on Thursday. I burn nine different mixes, flummoxed. Liana said things about the music controlling the atmosphere, things I didn't really understand.

I use '80s alternative as a jumping-off point, but I keep

being afraid that one of the songs I've chosen will send Liana running away from me like . . . well, like pretty much every other girl in the world.

One day, I am in the basement playing my Gibson ES-335. This was Alex Lifeson's guitar when he recorded "The Spirit of Radio," and while I've studied the tabs and can play the song, the exact sound keeps eluding me. I've written to Rush, care of their management, to ask about exactly what guitar effects Lifeson used in the recording of the song, and what effects were applied to the guitar track by the producer. Certainly a wah-wah pedal, but which one? Almost certainly a flanger, but every one is different.

Still, I am giving it a try in the basement while Chase tugs on the Bowflex. He enjoys it when I play Rush, or pretty much any hard rock or metal, while he works out. I am midway through the solo—one thing I love about Rush is the way the solos usually aren't overdubbed—when I stop because my heart's not in it.

"Come on, dude!" Chase, shirtless and sweating and sitting on the bench with his bandaged leg propped up, yells at me. "Two more reps!"

Reluctantly, I resume the solo, and when Chase has grunted his remaining reps out, I say, "I need your help."

Chase flashes me a smile. "Happy to help, bro. What do you need?"

"Well," I say as Chase wipes the sweat from his torso with a small towel and then begins wiping down the machine, "I am supposed to meet Liana, the girl from the hospital, on Thursday when I do my DJ thing at Espresso

Love, and I can't quite decide on the right mix to play."

"Uh-huh," Chase says. He shakes out his mane and puts on the gray, sleeveless Property of Carville Athletic Dept. XL shirt.

"We talked about '80s music, so I've been leaning heavily on that. I have a great mix focusing on Kirsty MacColl, but I'm worried that might send the wrong message, you know, since she and Steve Lillywhite got divorced and then she died tragically. Did you know the guy who killed her wasn't prosecuted, even though he was driving his boat in an area clearly designated as—"

"No, and I don't care, and neither will any normal girl, which is what your girlfriend seems to be, maybe. Well, if she likes you, I guess she's not normal by definition, but let's start by assuming that she's more normal than you are."

I laugh. "I think that's a safe assumption."

"Okay," he says. "So what message do you want the music to send?"

I don't want to send a message. I just want her to hear some music that she likes, and hopefully like me. "I don't know. I was thinking maybe I'd bring my guitar, you know, play a few—"

Chase holds up a hand. "No. Did you invite her to listen to you perform?"

"Well, no, but I thought, you know, my playing always goes over pretty well at the family reunions, and I like—"

"No. Freak alert. If you haven't scheduled a gig, you absolutely can't just show up and sing to her. She'll run from you like she thinks your freakishness is contagious."

I put the guitar down and sit on the floor, leaning against my amp.

"And try to stop doing that."

"Doing what?"

"Look at your hands," Chase says, and I look down and see that I was strumming the chords to The Smiths' "Please Please Please Let Me Get What I Want." I did not put this on any of the nine mixes I made, though it is on my mind somewhat. Even I recognize that inclusion of that song might sound desperate.

I stop strumming. "So which of my nine '80s alternative mixes should I use?"

"It doesn't freaking matter. Just . . . Okay, you talked about this music?"

"Yeah."

"Okay. Do not put on any songs that you talked about."

This eliminates six of my nine mixes, thus making my choice much easier, so I don't ask what Chase's rationale is. He is the expert here. "Uh, okay."

"What you want is music that can fade into the background if you need it to, you know, if the conversation gets interesting. But nothing that's obvious make-out music or anything. You should be able to listen to it if, by some miracle, the conversation lags."

He's smiling and starting to head up the stairs.

"But wait! You have to help me!"

"Music is your thing, Hank. You can do this. And I am not listening to a hundred and fifty songs so you can pick the best twenty-five."

He disappears up the stairs, leaving me alone in the basement.

I eventually decide on the Kirsty MacColl mix after all, because it might be kind of fun to play "What do these songs have in common" with songs by Talking Heads, The Smiths, Billy Bragg, The Pogues, The Rolling Stones, and Tom Tom Club, all of which feature Kirsty MacColl's backing vocals.

When I told Chase, he rolled his eyes at my suggestion that this might be fun, but didn't give me any helpful suggestions on how to talk to Liana. "Just figure out what she's interested in and pretend you're interested in it too," he said.

Mother was no more help. She told me "Just be yourself." I did not point out that this has proven spectacularly unsuccessful at getting girls within a five-foot radius of me in the past, except in elevators and at concerts, so it probably wouldn't work in this case either.

"Chase says I should pretend to like what she likes. I've done some research on recent developments in astronomy—"

Mother looked up from the sink, where she was washing her makeup off. "Do you have a concept of privacy? I just worked a twelve-hour day, and—forget it. Listen, sweetie, you know and I know that you have a lot of wonderful qualities, and you're going to make some lucky girl very happy."

I don't know this. I think this is one of those things people say as a kind of place marker in the conversation. This was a difficult concept for me to get, but Allie stressed a great deal that such place markers exist, and that "How are you doing?" is really just an extended hello and not a genuine inquiry. And so it is with these maternal assurances that her son is in some way attractive to the opposite sex.

"But," Mother continues, getting to the meaningful part of the conversation, "being a smooth conversationalist is not one of those qualities. Leave the insincerity and the game-playing to Chase—he's good at it. What's charming about you is your sincerity; don't try to overcome that."

Chase is male but does not face the same social challenges as I do. Mother is female but may be the only one who sees certain good qualities in me. Neither one of them is a reliable source. It occurs to me to call Allie, but her social skills lessons are a school-year-only service that is part of my 504 plan and not available during the summer. I am on my own.

Thursday arrives. I realize that I did not set a time with Liana, and that I therefore should spend the entire day in the coffee shop, from opening at six thirty a.m. to closing at eleven p.m. Chase tells me I am an idiot, and that Liana wouldn't be in the coffee shop in the morning because normal teenagers sleep late.

I have to work from eleven to three, so I will just head over to Espresso Love after work and hope she shows up between the hours of four and eleven. I don't know what I'll have for dinner, but I don't feel much like eating anyway.

I sell a Fender Stratocaster to a twelve-year-old boy holding a gift card he got for his birthday. I promise the guitarist from BloodFeaste that I can have his distortion pedal fixed before his gig on Saturday night. And when business slows down at one thirty (lunchtime, when weekend rockers wearing suits come in to look at guitars, is our busiest time), I ask the permission of Stan, the manager, and gingerly remove the Jazzmaster from the wall.

"It's kind of ironic," I tell Stan, who told me I'd be working for free until I died if anything happened to the Jazzmaster, and who is now watching me very closely, "that the Jazzmaster became the choice of musicians like Elvis Costello because it hadn't sold well and was therefore cheap. And now the popularity that came as a result of its low price has driven the price up."

Stan pushes his palms over the bald top of his head and runs them through the Ben Franklin–long hair that rings his baldness. "There's no way you're getting an additional discount on that guitar," he says, "so just stop trying."

I wasn't trying anything. I plug the guitar into a Marshall amp, tune it, and begin playing The Ventures' "Walk Don't Run."

Of course I've played this song before, but without the Jazzmaster's gigantic whammy bar, it's hard to make it sound right. As right as it sounds right now. Which is perfect. I finish "Walk Don't Run" and reluctantly place the Jazzmaster back on the wall.

"Don't sabotage any sales on that," Stan says, smiling. "If somebody wants it, you have to sell it to them."

"I know, Stan," I say. My fingers work chords even though my hands are without an instrument. Then I remember Chase telling me how weird this looks, so I stop. I stare at the guitar, mesmerized by its beauty. You can stare at inanimate objects, because it doesn't make them uncomfortable.

After work ends, I walk to Espresso Love. I do not drive

because I can walk pretty much everywhere I need to go. Also I don't have a license or a car.

I walk into Espresso Love, Kirsty MacColl–themed CD in hand. It occurs to me that I don't know what I'll do if I have to wait a long time for Liana. I didn't bring a book or a guitar catalog or anything to read until she arrives. If she arrives. I suppose I can always talk to Gary. He always has interesting anecdotes about musicians he met while tending bar at a dingy rock club in New York. I have heard most of them in the time I've been coming here, but listening to Gary's celebrity-vomit tales beats sitting by myself and thinking about all the various ways I can screw this up.

Fortunately I don't have to wait because Liana is sitting right near the window with an iced latte in front of her. "Hey!" she says, and smiles and waves.

"Hey," I say. I keep the CD in one hand and put my other in my pocket so I don't fidget too much. Liana sweeps her hair off her shoulders and waits for me. Her hair is brown and long with choppy shorter parts at the front, and I want to touch it.

"Hi," I say to her, and go over to the table. I don't touch her, of course. It's difficult enough to negotiate the rules of how normal people converse; when and how they hug, much less kiss or run their hands through each other's beautiful hair, is simply too advanced for me right now. Also I have a boner. I shrug and gesture to her with the CD. "Today's soundtrack," I say.

"Cool," she says. "Let's hear it!"

Behind the bar, Gary, the owner of Espresso Love, a

short, stocky man with a goatee, who is perpetually clad in a black T-shirt, calls out, "Hank! Got anything good for me to play? You've got to rescue me from this freaking Tori Amos." He points to the speakers, and one of the staff, a tall girl with shoulder-length red hair, who looks not unlike Tori Amos herself, rolls her eyes.

Gary allowed me to start playing music here largely because of this problem. "I hire 'em hot and crazy, which . . . I mean, I'm sorry, I have a weakness . . . but girls who look like that have absolute crap taste in music," he said to me one day, and I offered to help him out.

I throw the CD to him Frisbee-style. I practiced the throw in my room for quite a while, hoping to get it right. "Here you go." He catches it and pops it in the CD player.

I turn to walk to the table, and the Tori Amos girl bends down to pick up a spoon she's dropped. I look. Tramp stamp.

I look back over at Liana, who is looking at me looking at Tori's lower back. I wonder if I should tell her about how I check for the tramp stamp, but I decide we'll be better off if we just pretend that whole thing never happened.

"I'm back," I say, and sit across from her. The sunlight slants in from outside, making her right half seem like it's illuminated. I will myself not to stare at her. It's difficult. When someone is beautiful, you just want to look at them. I hear Van Halen's "Beautiful Girls" in my mind and start chording it.

"So," Liana says, "we meet again. . . ." She grins. "How's your summer so far?" She looks at my hands, and I stop playing.

"Is this the Pogues?" Liana asks, saving me from giving a truthful answer to that impossible question. A girl paid attention to me for the first time. So far, it's the best summer of my life.

"Yes!" I say. I'm about to talk about Kirsty MacColl's backing vocals, but that will pretty much blow the entire game.

"Okay. Got it. I'm sure I'll be able to figure this out," she says, smiling.

"Hank! Your first decaf Americano is up!" Gary calls out from the bar.

"Did you order two coffees?" Liana asks, looking at me the way kids do in the cafeteria, like I've got no place being here. Or anywhere.

I swallow hard and nod. "Yeah. See, I always drink the first one too fast . . ." I stop talking, wishing I'd only ordered one, and that Gary hadn't shouted my order across the room. Not that I actually ordered. I get the same thing every time I come in here. "It's bizarre." I look at her. "It's okay. I know it's weird." She gives me another long look. I get up and collect my coffee.

"Dude, you're reminding me of my misspent youth," Gary says. "One time after a Pogues concert—" He looks over at the table where Liana is sitting. She gives a little wave. This is an adorable gesture. "Sorry, dude. Didn't realize you had company. She's cute!"

"Yes she is," I say, and return to the table. "So here's my first drink. He'll make my second one in about five minutes. I know it's kind of a freak-show thing to do."

She laughs. "It's not a freak-show thing. . . ." She tucks her hair behind her ears. "It's brilliant. I mean, all the time I have to nurse my coffee so it lasts longer. Why not just guzzle one and then savor the next?"

I smile at her. "That's exactly my point," I tell her. We sit there not saying much while she fiddles with her wallet. Or the thing she uses as her wallet. The silence makes me nervous.

"Shane MacGowan was recently voted the ugliest man in rock and roll. I think maybe Stiv Bators deserved consideration, but I don't know if you had to be alive to—" I say, and Liana is smiling. I'm playing the chords to the Pogues' "If I Should Fall from Grace with God" along with the CD, and Liana is staring at my hands.

"You always hear music, don't you?" she says.

"Uh. Yeah. One more freak-show thing, I guess."

"I don't think it's freakish. I mean, it's . . . it just shows that you're passionate about it."

She's just said *passionate*. I have the urge to grab my skull to stop it from exploding. Instead, I take a big gulp of coffee that's too hot.

CHAPTER 7
LIANA

"How's your brother?" It seems like the right thing to ask Hank, given how we met and everything. Plus it distracts me from looking too much at his lake-water eyes. They have rings, like a planet, but I can't tell him that. I also can't tell him that I think I get him, how his voice rises and dips with so much feeling. All that passion and depth make him kind of nervous, which at first was unsettling, but now only makes me more curious about him.

"My brother?" Hank furrows his brows and wriggles his fingers around. I've noticed he's always doing that—shifting his fingers, not fidgeting really, more playing chords. I wish I could hear what he's playing. "Chase is fine. Still fine. He's always fine. He's healthy enough to do his usual weights and lifting . . ." He stares at me and stops his description of Chase's workout. "He's pretty fit," he says, and then looks like he wants to take the comment back.

"Yeah," I agree because it's the truth, and then, just to make it clear I am not fixating on Hank's hot brother, I add, "My dad's okay too, in case you were wondering."

Hank nods. "Your mom said so, so I figured . . ."

I exhale sharply through my nose and push my hair from my face. "Well, she always says that, so you can't really go by her view of how he is."

Hank nods but then says, "I don't think I know what you mean."

I sigh and look out the window. Melissa Winkle and [insert name of boy here] are far enough away that I can't make out the girl's face, can't see much of him except to know they're having fun and get to kiss each other and hold hands and wander around being a couple. I focus back on Hank. "It's just . . . it's a pattern he does, this health crisis and then back to life as usual on planes and traveling all the time, and so what? I mean, if you're not going to change, then your pattern becomes . . ."

"A big wheel that keeps on turning," Hank says. "You find references to the big wheel turning not only in Creedence songs, but also in Steve Miller, Journey—I suppose it could be the sun, but it's kind of interesting that the wheel is a Buddhist image that turns up in all these western rock songs."

I sip my coffee and wonder why Hank always has to revert back to music. It's like a tic or something. Like the way my mother shakes her foot when she crosses her leg. She can't stop it. I find it so annoying I can't look at her when she does it. I study Hank's expression. He studies me. It's

65

like we're trying to figure out how and why we're here, or maybe I've just been spending too much time at the science lab. "I don't think I know any of those songs," I tell him. "Are they on the mix?"

He shakes his head. "They don't fit the theme."

"Right. The theme." My thumb goes to my tattoo, and I trace the familiar hip skin, imagining the blue sphere.

"But I guess songs about wheels turning would be a good mix too. Not that the mix we're listening to now is necessarily connected by a lyrical theme. I mean, well, they could be connected by a lyrical theme, but they aren't necessarily connected that way." He swipes his hands though his hair. The hair looks soft, not brushed or anything, but he's one of those guys with naturally soft hair, who probably has no idea of its appeal, which only makes him more appealing. What's the scientific name for that? Being clueless?

I laugh at his rambling, at the fact that he rambled and then cut himself off. "You're not going to give it away? You're obviously dying to tell me."

He shakes his head and continues to chord some unheard song on his coffee cup. "I do want to tell you, but I'm just afraid—" he says, and it comes out all mysterious. He's like the tortured artist I've always wanted to discover. The kind of guy who stays awake at night wandering the streets and thinking about you and then sitting in some funky warehouse writing songs about you. I imagine him there tonight, lying belly down on the concrete floor of the warehouse, immune to the coldness because he's so intent on immortalizing the hurricane of feelings he has for me.

"Afraid of what? That we'll have nothing to talk about if the game is over?" I joke, but Hank doesn't hear the joke in my voice and looks like I dumped coffee on his head. "I mean, not that I expect that."

Hank looks at me for a long time. "Really?" he says.

I'm not sure how to answer this, so I tune in to the music. "Wait. Is that . . . What the hell's his name? Bill somebody?"

"Billy Bragg!" Hank says, and starts miming playing along.

I listen for a minute. "I'm going to need another few songs before I can guess the theme. The first one was really rowdy, but this one's kind of sad. It's . . ." Just then, the line "Something waiting for the worms to claim" jumps out, wraps a cold hand around my heart, and squeezes. Everything's about to come rushing to the surface, but fortunately, Hank comes to my rescue.

"Okay, okay, I'll tell you," he says. "It's Kirsty MacColl." He starts talking, stuff about producers and backing vocals and somebody power boating where they shouldn't have, and I can't really follow it. It's as though he's reciting liner notes from the inside of one of my parents' albums. The ones I look at sometimes when I'm poking around, rummaging through the basement. Those albums are chucked away, boxed in no particular order, along with ancient letters and photographs my parents refuse to acknowledge. So while Hank might not be saying what I want to hear right now, while he might be spewing facts or fictions about music history, I'm glad for the distraction.

CHAPTER 8
HANK

A couple days, a whole lot of coffee, and one probably-too-long lecture about Kirsty MacColl later, Liana and I are sitting at our same table and drinking our same drinks and trying to get the conversational ball rolling.

I've brought a mix with what I think is a pretty obvious theme: it's Hanks, a collection of songs by Hank Williams and his grandson, Hank Williams III. I am not a fan of Hank Williams, Jr.

Hank Williams III is still putting music out, but I've only included songs from his first two releases because I don't listen to music recorded after 2003.

2003 is the year when I first really got into music. I enjoyed the way I could put headphones on and shut out everything that was happening—the nattering relatives, Mother, even the seemingly endless parade of casseroles and cookies that passed through the house. It was a weird, confusing time, when all the normal routines in the house went completely out the window, when everything I thought I knew or understood changed. And the song, as Led Zeppelin said, remains the same. Unless you're listening to an old vinyl copy and putting new scratches and pops in it every time, you can listen to, for example, "The Ocean" one thousand times and it will always sound exactly the same.

So my mix doesn't feature any music from Hank III's most recent album. I am nervous because the theme is so obvious that it won't make much of a game to figure it out. Also because so many people say they like "everything but country," and here I have two country artists. Hank Williams is singing "Settin' the Woods on Fire," and neither of us is talking. We're just listening to the song. I'm afraid Liana's going to hate it, and I can't stand the silence.

This is what Allie used to make us do when we first started social skills group: we had to chuck this little foam ball with the name of a prescription drug printed on the side at each other, and the person who caught the ball had to continue the conversation. So after a full two minutes and thirty-eight seconds of silence, I ball up a napkin and chuck it at her. I know it was two minutes and thirty-eight seconds because that's the entire length of "Settin' the Woods on Fire."

"Why'd you throw this at me?" Liana rolls the napkin ball back to me.

"Well, that's how you do it," I say, and send it back to her. "You throw the ball, or in this case, the napkin, at somebody, and then they have to speak."

"So, what, we like, talk and play a rousing game of napkin catch?" She grins and twists her hair up into a coil with a pencil from her bag. The pencil has teeth marks on it. I get slightly lost in the vision of the pencil surrounded by her mouth.

"So is this like, demented flirting or just a way to pass time?" she asks while she rockets the ball my way.

My impulse when she mentions demented flirting is to run from the café. But I have the napkin, and I have to say something. "No, uh, it's, uh, I just, it's a kind of an exercise. For when you're having trouble talking." I fling the napkin back at her before I stammer any longer.

"I wasn't aware we were having that issue," Liana says, and cups the ball in her palm.

I breathe in, letting the air-conditioning fill my lungs. I hate the heat—August's heat seems to have arrived early in July this year—but the constant chill of the air-conditioning makes me feel stuffy and muddle-headed. I mean more so than usual. I got very stuffed up at work today, where Stan keeps the air-conditioning set to arctic so that the humidity doesn't warp the necks of the guitars. Also, Stan wouldn't let me near the Jazzmaster because someone called about it. If someone's interested in buying it, Stan keeps it in its spot, clean and untouched, so as not to put off the buyer.

"It's your turn," Liana says, and chucks the ball at me. "And P.S.: just so you're aware, sitting in silence for the length of a song isn't not having anything to say. It's just"—she looks out the window and then looks harder, seeing something or someone—"it's just chilling out for a second."

"Or one hundred and fifty-eight seconds." I feel kind of at sea, but the napkin ball is in my hand, so I have to talk. "There's this beautiful guitar at the shop. Vintage sea green Fender Jazzmaster. It's a beautiful guitar. Stan . . ." I pause to see if she's listening, which you can tell usually by how someone looks at you. Her eyes are focused on mine. "Stan's the owner. He sometimes lets me take it down and play a surf instrumental. . . ." My hands automatically start playing "Walk Don't Run." "And it sounds amazing. I mean, not because of my playing or anything, but because the guitar is just . . . perfect."

"It sounds cool," she says. She looks out the window at people going by. A man with a dog. A couple of kids on bikes. An old man with a cane. I remember that old guy sitting at the table near us in the hospital cafeteria. Then I wonder why I'm thinking about him.

"Remember that old crying guy?" I ask her, and quickly throw her the ball. She smiles and catches it.

"In the cafeteria?" Liana nods. "He was so sad. It's awful." She rolls the ball back to me.

At first I'm terrified that she means the music, but then I remember she's talking about the guy crying. "Yeah," I say. This is a high-quality conversation filler. Liana sips her coffee and squints out the window at a guy and a girl about our age. They could be brother and sister. Or cousins. Or a couple. It's hard to tell. They're holding hands, though. I guess that makes them a couple. Or very strange siblings. "I mean," she says, "not just that he was crying. Being that alone."

I nod. I still have the ball, but I don't want to talk about being alone. On my "Hanks" mix, Hank Williams is singing about being so lonesome he could cry. "Yeah," I say again, and again it appears to be the correct thing to say.

I take a sip of my coffee because I don't know what else to say. The Tori Amos girl with the tramp stamp is staring at us. Maybe she thinks *we're* cousins. Or a couple. Or maybe she just sees a family resemblance between me and Chase, whom she went out with after he stopped in for coffee the other day, worked his magic, and got her digits.

Silence invades again, and this time Hank Williams III fills it up. I listen, watch Liana's face to see if she likes what she hears, and let my fingers move on my coffee cup. I'm playing an imaginary Dobro. I look down, embarrassed, and stop. I don't actually know how to play a Dobro. I'm about to tell her something about Hank Williams III, but I don't have the ball.

"It's okay," she says. "You know, you can actually talk without the ball. I saw you were about to say something there."

I don't say anything, and gesture for the ball, which she throws at me. It misses and lands in my coffee. "Well, I like the rules," I say. "I guess it just keeps . . . It makes things easy to negotiate."

I'm fishing the napkin ball out of my coffee cup and trying to squeeze the coffee out of it into another napkin. I realize I could just crumple another napkin up, but Liana's already talking, so I guess the exercise is over. "Not me." Liana shakes her head and touches the condensation on her plastic cup. "I like being surprised." She thinks. "Being caught off guard. Otherwise . . . it's . . ."

I wait for her to say more but she doesn't. "Otherwise it's what?"

"Nothing." She shakes her head. "Maybe I just mean science. I was in the lab before, and it's just—I can know the distance from Earth to any given planet, but . . ." Her voice fades out and she puts her fingers near her hip. "You can't know everything before you start a project. Otherwise you're not really testing anything." She looks at me. "Sorry. Does this make sense?"

I shrug. "Not really." I realize Chase probably would have lied and said he was following what Liana was talking about, and I wonder if I've messed up. I'm taking Mother's advice and being myself, but I have to balance this against everyone else's advice of blending in. I pause, take a deep breath, and try to remember Allie's advice about letting people get a word in edgewise and asking questions and listening to the answers. "How's your project going?"

"It's slow going," she says. "I mean, in a lot of ways it's tedious, but it's just such a relief to be able to spend all my time doing what I'm interested in instead of being forced to march through *A Tale of Two Cities* or whatever else they're making me do in my other classes."

"I know," I say. "When I'm in class, I dream about guitars, but when I'm selling guitars, I don't think about trigonometry."

She laughs. "Exactly." The song ends, and the next one, "Five Shots of Whiskey," begins.

"What's the project about, anyway?" I ask.

"Technically?" she asks, and I shrug. "A star census. I'm sort of explaining why stars twinkle." She twists her mouth to the side. "God, that sounds dumb. But it's complicated. See, the moon and planets don't twinkle."

"How about *not* technically?" I ask her. This makes her laugh. She chews on the sugar in her coffee. *Try to find common interests,* Allie says in my head. *Find out what she likes and pretend you like it too,* Chase adds. "The sugar never melts all the way," I say. "That could be a scientific experiment right there."

She crunches more. "True. But this is for college credit, if you're asking. My parents felt that I'd have a better shot at getting into a top place if I had extra credit in advanced science." She pauses. "Which I already do . . . but . . . hey, it's better than working here." She looks at Gary behind the counter, then reconsiders. "But maybe if I did work here, you'd provide the soundtrack."

"So you like it?" I point up as though the music is in the air somewhere.

Liana pauses and listens for a moment. Hank Williams III is singing about how it's all gone wrong since you've been gone.

"Oh God, that is just about the saddest song I've ever heard."

She pauses and listens, and Hank III continues to bemoan his fate: abandoned by someone he loves, alone, and turning to alcohol to try to ease his misery. I don't have any personal experience with this, but to judge by Chase's misadventures with the bottle, drinking appears to actually cause a great

74

deal of misery. At least in the morning, or in Chase's case, even early afternoon.

Liana is looking at her lap. I don't know what she's thinking. She breathes deeply, runs a hand across her face, and looks up at me. "Did you do that on purpose?"

"I, uh . . . I didn't . . . I mean, I put the song on the CD on purpose, but in terms of trying to cause a specific emotion or something, no. As a matter of fact . . ." Chase would tell me never to reveal what I'm about to reveal, while Mother would tell me to be myself. I guess being myself includes not pretending that I understand things I don't understand.

I'm about to tell her. I open my mouth.

The door to the café opens, and someone walks in. The couple, or possibly very strange siblings, from outside. The boy is wearing a fake-vintage AC/DC shirt. The girl is wearing a shirt that appears to be several sizes too small for her and that reveals the tramp stamp on her lower back. It is a curlicue of thorns, or possibly barbed wire, that is, to judge by the tramp stamps I've seen, somewhat of a tattoo cliché. Liana's face changes when she sees them come in, and suddenly she's standing up.

"Look," she says, "I have to go."

I wonder if she's angry because of the music. I wonder if there were signs I couldn't read and I went speeding the wrong way down a one-way street again. I dig into my bag.

"I have a British Invasion mix if you prefer that," I tell her. "I know a lot of people don't like country music. I just . . . it's Hank Williams. My namesake. And his grandson."

Liana stares past me at the couple, who have their hands in each other's pockets. It doesn't look comfortable. The boy casts a glance over his shoulder and gives a big grin.

"No, Hank, it's not country music. Only that . . ." Her voice is wavy, like she's using the wah-wah pedal. "I just can't . . ." She squeezes her wallet thing and bites her lip. "Can we take a rain check?"

"It's sunny," I joke, and point to outside even though by now I completely understand what she means. As a kid I thought it really meant it was raining. "But yeah. Of course. Tomorrow?"

She heads for the door. "Tomorrow. As usual."

We have a usual? This seems hopeful, even though she is running away from me as so many girls have done before. I look at the couple. The guy who smiled at us still has his hand in the girl's back pocket. He starts kneading her butt ostentatiously, like he's planning on making baked goods out of it. "Tomorrow," I agree.

Liana shifts her bag and chews on her lip. "By the beach, okay? On the path by the food shop. Around eight."

"Okay," I tell her. This is what people call mixed signals. She got upset by the song, maybe because she doesn't like songs about drinking, and then she left, but not without agreeing to see me again. I have no idea what I've done wrong, or if it was even me. *When you don't know, it's okay to ask.* "What happened? Did I do something wrong?" Almost certainly, but if you tell me what it is, I can avoid doing it again.

She shakes her head and glances at the couple one more time. "No. Not really. Look, I'll explain another time."

She all but runs out of the coffee shop, and I think I should probably explain later, too.

CHAPTER 9
LIANA

After lab work the next day, I open the side door of the house and drop my bag and shoes in the hallway before going in so I don't get any sand or summer dirt on the floors. Dust and grime are my mother's enemies, and I don't want her wrath on me. Especially because it's not a wrath as in yelling, pestering, demanding. She's intricate that way. Even though I want to leave my sweatshirt on the floor, I hang it up on the brass hook by the bench. The same bench I sat on every morning when I learned how to tie my shoes. The same bench on which my father will sling his briefcase and laptop when he eventually comes home from Wherever, USA, and the same bench from which my mother will collect said items and put them neatly into the shared study down the hall.

I let my hair down from its coil and flip through the mail on the tray. No letters from Cat in Italy. Nothing but bills and credit card offers. I look around the living room and head for the kitchen. The house is over a century old, so it's got lots of smaller rooms. Not an open plan like the modern houses around here. At Cat's house you can yell from the kitchen into the living room, and crane your neck forward in the den and see practically the whole downstairs. Our house is like a series of rabbit warrens.

The best part of coming home is the same thing as the worst part: the house is always the same. The kitchen has a properly stocked fridge—enough greens for a hearty salad but not enough that they wind up wilted and soggy if they're unused—the laundry is folded and left in baskets outside my parents' room and my room, the wood floors are shiny, and the air smells like whatever my mother is baking.

"Chocolate chip banana bread," she says when I enter the kitchen. Her face is round, full moon–like, but she's a tiny woman, so she's always seems like she could topple over. She's wearing maroon linen pants that dwarf her. "It'll be ready in a bit. It's whole wheat."

"God forbid we have white flour anymore," I joke, and open the fridge door, onto which all of my report cards are taped. We have to use tape because the fridge is stainless steel and shiny but doesn't accept magnets. The letters are universally vowels—that is, all A's, save for my independent study in chemistry, which is an A-minus. I joked with my parents that the minus was for variety, but they didn't see the humor.

I look around the shelves for something to eat, but I don't want anything. I'm just biding time until I can go to my room without Mom thinking I'm angry at her. In truth, I'm not, even though her incessant baking drives me crazy. She's either baking or in her study. This week alone has brought a wave of carrot muffins, lavender tea biscuits, and bite-size caramel swirl brownies I gave to Hank to take to work. We can't eat or keep all of the things she makes, or they just go stale. The freezer is filled with things already. She bakes as though she's preparing food for a much larger family.

"Something wrong?" she asks while she slops the dough into a bread pan. She's always been a baker. I suspect she finds the predictability comforting, the scientific aspects of it—how eggs are a binding agent, how sodium bicarbonate makes dough rise.

"Remember when I used to help you stir?" I mime the action and she smiles.

She nods for a minute, and then a certain look comes over her, and she gets back to business.

"Nothing's wrong," I tell her, even though it's not true.

She brightens. "How's the lab work?"

I tilt my head forward, seeing her through my bangs. "Cool." She waits for more. "I'm predicting twinkling." She nods, encouraging me, every bit the high school guidance counselor. "So I have to do a star census. At night, obviously. And I have to do it at different times—like when there's a full moon or a partial."

"So you'll do that tonight, then?" She wipes her spotless hands on her hips.

I nod. I wasn't exactly planning on it, but maybe Hank will be game for it. I watch my mother check on the banana bread, holding the pan, as though she's cradling a baby, to tap the bottom the way she always checks bread to see if it's done. I feel guilty for leaving. "Save a piece for me for later, okay?"

"Of course. And I'll freeze a loaf for Dad. He had to switch flights. Now he's not due back until the weekend." She keeps stirring while I head for the stairs.

I take the steps slowly, wishing I hadn't bolted from Espresso Love. Wishing I hadn't seen Fiona Clark and Pren Stevens. Not that I like him anymore or anything. But seeing their hands in each other's pockets. Knowing he was going to kiss her. It was too much. All that longing that pushes a kiss to the surface. All the pent-up lust or love or just wanting to not be alone.

But if my experiment is going to work—not the one I'm doing in the lab, but the one I'm performing on my own self—I have to forget kissing. For the whole summer. How else can I determine the whys, and how best to proceed in the fall when I'm back at my locker waiting for another note?

I'm halfway up the stairs when Mom calls to me. "Liana!"

"What?" I poke my head over the side of the railing.

"You dropped this." My mother's apron is spotless. Probably she doesn't need to wear one at all, but does it just because that's what you're supposed to do. She hands me my wallet case. My slut note is clearly visible through the outside. I take it from her, and as our hands meet, we lock eyes.

If she asks me about it, I decide right then, I will tell her. I will confess to my kisses and ask her what it means, or what she thinks it means. I wait. "I'd better get that other loaf in if we want to eat some later!" She takes a deep breath and turns away.

"I'm going out in, like, ten minutes," I tell her. "Just so you know."

She nods but doesn't face me. "Will you be out late?"

Define late, I think, but all I say is, "It depends on Hank."

Exactly what depends on Hank I have no idea. I'll meet him by the beach tonight and let him complete his sentence from yesterday. I know he had more to say and that I cut him off and that if Cat were here she'd say that this was my subconscious trying to play hard to get. Trying to make Hank feel something for me by being out of reach. But if she were here I'd counter that thought with this: Neither my conscious self nor my unconscious self should be trying to lure anyone. In my experience, luring leads to liking, and liking leads to kissing, and then suddenly you're opening your locker and finding out people think you're a slut.

"I got you something," Hank says as soon as I'm within shouting distance of Sam & Nate's, the beach store that bumps into the shore. They sell your usual sandy fare: every number of SPF, poor-quality flip-flops, salty chips, and bags of ice for bonfire parties. During Beachfest, the annual summer concert and all-day party, the store is crammed with T-shirts and hats, each one advertising something.

"Oh yeah?" I look at him and then up at the night sky. Waxing crescent. I swing my bag and say, "I brought my notebook. For a star census. "

"You're doing homework?" Hank walks toward me, his

81

hands wrapped around a bottle in a brown bag. Just what I don't need. Drinking, beach, summer, and a boy are not going to help me in my experiment, so I start to shake my head.

"No."

"Not homework?" Hank's closer now, close enough to offer me the drink in the paper bag.

"I can't drink tonight, Hank." Plus, I'm not the biggest drinker anyway. I squint up at the sky, checking to see if it's even worth documenting what's up there tonight.

Hank stands close to me. Very close. I can see his light eyes, nearly phosphorescent. "I thought you'd like it." He sounds deeply saddened. "I just thought . . ."

I take the bag from him and peer inside. "Oh!" I remove the bottle and cap and swig hard. "Root beer in a glass bottle. You remembered!"

Hank gives me the sweetest small smile. "I remembered." It's as though he can't believe it himself.

Where the road ends and the path through the dunes to the beach begins, right next to the signs warning us not to dig deep holes, is the first flyer of the summer for Beachfest. I point at it. "Check it out," I say. "Alligator Teeth on the main stage. Great party band."

"Mmm," Hank says. He's not really looking. Maybe he's contemplating the stars. Or me. Or not.

"Not a funk fan?" I ask. The wind whips my hair into my face, and I have to keep swatting at it so I don't wind up chewing on it.

"Oh, no. I, you know, *Mothership Connection*, *One Nation Under a Groove*, I dig it." Hank shoves his hands in his pockets, and I wonder if he's chording still, but I can't see the motion. I like knowing what his hands are doing, though. He stares at the Beachfest poster, the big microphone, the two stages drawn in ragged red and black, bonfires burning in the background. It's the biggest deal of the summer around here; one big night o'fun before the reality of fall hits.

"You're gonna play the second stage this year?" I ask, because I assume he is. He's studying the poster still but suddenly turns to me.

"Am I . . . wait. What?" Hank looks as though he just tuned in.

"Well, I mean you play music, right?" I sip my soda.

"Yeah, but—"

"I just figured you already were . . ." I lick the drip of root beer from where it splashed on my hand. "So why not? The second stage would be a great way for you to get your music out there, you know, spread the word." Then I wonder if maybe I'll regret this; unleashing Hank onto the world for everyone to hear, to want, to want to take away from me.

"I . . . that's . . ."

"A great idea?" Because it is, even if it feels risky. Who am I to keep him as my own personal best secret? Besides, I'm sure he's already known all over his school as some musician or closeted musician, so why not burst out?

"Yes." Hank is very sure. His voice is loud. "That's exactly what it is. I'll send them a demo."

"Cool," I say. "And I'll be there to listen." I say it and wonder if it's true. A lot could happen between now and then. Many days left of my experiment. Many kiss-free zones, many nights and songs to sit through without ever touching anyone's lips to mine. I shrug to myself. However, as the equation of my experiment would show, kissing = potential slutdom = more kissing = inevitably bolting. So no kissing, no bolting, right?

We walk a little ways down the path toward the beach, and when we're right in front of the changing rooms—which are really just wooden slatted structures with portable potties built in—Hank suddenly stops.

"I have to—" He looks pained to admit it.

"Go to the . . ." I gesture to the sign that reads MEN. The stick figure on it has one leg raised in the running position as if it is in dire need of the facilities.

"Yeah. Sorry."

He leaves and I stand there in the warm air, holding my seemingly illicit bottle of something in a brown bag, laughing to myself that Hank is sweet enough to apologize that he needs to do something as basic as pee. I find myself swaying slightly as the wind blows against my lower legs.

"Liana, hey!" I turn, starting to walk away because I think it's Hank, but it's not. It's Jett Alterman—otherwise known as Musician #4 in the movie version of my life—and he's not alone. My heart turns on itself. I grip the bottle harder as though it's Hank's hand. A few other guys and a herd of girls walk in a big group past where I am, heading for the far end of the beach, away from the pier. I wave hello. "It's bonfire time," Jett says, his eyes half closed as usual, some girl's hand on his sleeve. "You in?"

Am I in? No. "I can't," I say. Jett looks around as if to

suggest that if I have other plans, they can't be great. "I have a . . . My friend." I sound silly, all alone here, and realize I look lame. I start a few sentences and then Hank's out of the bathroom, his hair in his eyes, his shirt rumpled like he just woke up, all very adorable and innocent. Hank doesn't even seem to care that Jett or his buddies are milling around not introducing themselves. A few of the girls laugh, and I wonder if they're laughing at me. One of them was in APS with me, but dropped out. Not many survive the planetary sciences at Melville. Senior year it'll just be me and three other kids total.

Jett chucks a Frisbee up the path.

"Why don't you bring your—ah—whatever he is, to the pits?" He points to them as his group starts to thin out, each one hauling a cooler, a bag of charcoal, striped towels—your typical beach fun.

Hank looks confused, and I open my mouth to ask him if he wants to go, but nothing comes out. I want to explain exactly who Hank is to Jett, and what I'm doing, and why I have no desire go to some lame bonfire where the point is to waste the next five hours so that someone can hook up with someone else.

"If you want to go, you can," Hank says. He looks at the sandy path and then tries to focus on me.

I shake my head. "No thanks," I say to Jett. "I'm kind of. My . . ." I say again, but Jett's already moved on. He casts one look back to me—to us—and I realize he sees it all wrong. Me—the kissing bandit, with a bottle of who knows what, with an unknown and unnamed boy, on the beach at night. But it's not like that.

* * *

Later, Hank and I are balancing precariously on the edge of the pier. Barefooted and giddy from the sugary root beer, I make sure my notebook, full of notes about how many stars I can see tonight through my star finder, is safe from sea spray.

"A star is a point of light," I say in my giving-a-science-speech voice. "It's so far away that even the largest telescope can't show the star's disk." I wait for Hank to interrupt me. He just takes it all in like he's recording it for future reference. I tie my hair back with the black elastic I keep around my wrist. "The atmosphere changing between the star and your eye causes starlight to twinkle."

"Twinkle, twinkle," Hank repeats. His whole body is supported only by his heels. He leans over the water.

He looks like he might fall in. "Watch out!" I yell to him.

He seems to ignore me, playing chords on his thighs while watching me dangle my legs over the edge. "Don't ever put 'Under the Boardwalk' on a mix for me."

"Oh, because I was just about to make you a mix?" I grin up at him. His hair is blowing in many directions at once. "I don't like that song anyway. It's too cotton candy and sticky Popsicles and hiding out away from the sun. Actually, that doesn't sound too bad." Hank shrugs. His balance is worrying. "Really, don't fall. I don't want to have to jump in and rescue you."

He moves closer to me. "You know I actually can't swim?"

This sends a jolt of panic through me. Yet it also fits

his image. Not so much the typical hero; he's the one off to the sidelines, maybe calling for help if someone's drowning. "Well, no one's drowning."

"A girl at school nearly drowned last year," he says, breaking the light mood we had going.

"That's awful." Did he write songs about it? Did he never learn to swim because he's got some scar on his back I can't see? It's all very intense and unusual and appealing.

"Everyone at school was running around, crazy. Like that song 'Hysteria.' But then she was fine." Hank nods. "Her locker had, like, a thousand cards plastered on it. Flowers and stuff."

I swallow this and the ocean air. The salty night and Hank's candor about everything make me feel like layers of paint are being pulled off of me. "Why is it that no one ever sends unsigned *good* notes?" I ask him. I stand up and go to where he is, balanced on the pier's corner. Behind us, the beach is coming alive with shouts of revelry; the summer bonfires flare up like comets. "I mean, no one ever sends a note your way that's all, *Hey you are so smart,* without trying to coerce you into doing something or getting something in return." Then I remember that there are secret admirer notes, unsigned, but leaving you swooning. I scuff my feet against the sand on the pier.

"I don't get any notes," Hank says, but he doesn't appear to mourn this. It's just a statement.

"Well, you're lucky, I guess." I wait for him to ask me more, to query why, but he doesn't. So in the open dark air, with him avoiding eye contact, I explain, "I get them.

87

Sometimes. Sometimes my friend Cat will ask if I did the assignment. Or if I want to go for pizza later. But then . . ." He turns to me, watching me. I look at the ocean below. It's high tide, so the water's close, rising up the pilings, maybe five feet below us. "Then I get this note, right? And it just says . . ." I consider jumping into the water to avoid this next word.

"'Got a box full of letters, think you might like to read . . .'" Hank sings. "Jeff Tweedy. Wilco. Good song."

"Hank, listen to me. I'm not talking about songs, here," I say, and my voice is suddenly scratchy. "I'm saying . . ." Hank stops humming and forces himself to stop chording. "All my note said was *slut*, okay? Like that's supposed to sum up who I am." I could cry. Or not. I could fling myself into the water. Or not. But I don't do either. I just wait to see what Hank the Intense, Funny, Odd has to say.

He thinks, turning his back to the wind so his shirt billows out. His head and legs look tiny, and his torso looks wide, like he's a sail. "But what if it's not everyone?" he wonders. "It could just be one person. Then you would only be a slut in *their* eyes." He hums "In Your Eyes" by Peter Gabriel.

Such a simple thing to say. The perfect thing. The only good response. I want to grab his hand and pull him into the water. Kiss him on the way down. "Good album," I say, staying right where I am. "I like 'Red Rain.'"

He nods and starts to walk back to the beach path. "'Red Red Wine.'"

"'Cigarettes and Chocolate Milk,'" I add, grabbing my bag and following.

"Rufus Wainwright?" he guesses.

I nod at the guess and at his matter-of-fact way of assessing my note. We're side by side, walking on the sandy gritty pavement away from town toward the three-season cottages on numbered streets. "Here." I hold the note out to him. It flaps in between my fingers and he takes it from me, and I can almost feel him sucking the word from me, like it's all his now, his to figure out or deal with, even though I know it's not. Hank holds it up in the dim streetlight, trying to read it with the help of the moon.

"Now, if only the moon twinkled"—he suggests and I laugh—"then it would be easier to read."

"It's just the one word," I say to him. I still can't believe I told him. That I showed him. It's like being naked in some ways. And that he didn't try to maul me or run away.

"So that's it?" He lowers himself down into one of the green benchs at the side of the pier. "That's your secret? The thing you couldn't say at the café?"

I shake my head. "Yeah, it's fine. That's it." The lie doesn't show on my face because by now I've perfected a poker face that would rule Vegas.

"Good," he says, falling for it. He plucks at one of my tank top straps and it snaps against my skin with a pinch. I wince but he doesn't care. He just says, "Come on."

Hank's house is a Monopoly house come to life. A squat blue square on the corner of Second and Twenty-first. "'Where the Streets Have No Name.'" He points to the number signs and kicks open the unlocked front door.

"'Home Sweet Home . . .'" Hank croons a melody and mutters, "Mötley Crüe," before shedding his footwear on a woven rug that looks like sunsets—all oranges and reds overlapping.

I cross my arms and hold on to my bag while checking out the place. It's your standard beach cottage, with a two-sided main room and a kitchen I can see way at the back of the house. Cat's family owns one and rents it out in the summer, so I can imagine the rest of the floor plan. One side of the main room is a living room filled with furniture that looks like it's seen better days. Or better years. "Have you lived here long?" I ask. Maybe they just stay here in the summer. Most of the cottages don't have heat, which would make winter more than a little cold.

"A while," Hank says, not committing to any distinct time, and motioning for me to come into the kitchen.

The dining room, which is the other part of the main room, is more a tumble of clutter. The table is littered with books and piles of papers, receipts flutter like winged things, and even the floor has a few stray plates and a pair of glasses. I pick them up. "Here, someone could step on them."

Hank nods. "Yeah, usually I'm that someone. They're my mom's. She always forgets them. Then she comes home and screams around the house looking for them."

"In a million years my mother would never scream."

Hank leans on the doorjamb between the clutter and the kitchen. "Too busy baking?" I grin. He gets it.

The kitchen is warm, glowing from a red light fixture that hangs too low over a Formica table. Cereal boxes are lined up on the windowsill—Wheaties, Cheerios, All-Bran, and Lucky Charms, which Hank snags before he leads me upstairs.

"So, you like sugary cereals?" I ask when what I want to do is inquire why he's taking me up to the bedroom level, if maybe now that he knows what my note said, he thinks I am what it said.

Hank stops on the stairs, his upper body hunched over because of the low ceiling. "I don't like cereal at all. It's too . . . boxed? That's not the right way to explain it, but it's flaky or little balls or things that dissolve." He chords on the Lucky Charms box.

"And Lucky Charms escapes the cereal definition because . . ." We take the steps slowly. They creak underfoot, worn down in the middle from decades of different feet doing exactly the same thing.

We stop in the hallway. The walls are entirely covered in dark wood paneling. "I don't eat the cereal part. Only the marshmallows." Hank slides his fingers under the box lid and rustles the plastic bag open. "Try them, seriously."

"I've had them before." I peer behind him into the biggest bedroom, his parents', probably. Queen-size bed, dresser, oval mirror. I can't see anything else from this angle. Hank sees me looking in there and immediately pulls me out of the hallway and into one of the other bedrooms.

"They're really good," he says, still focused on the cereal. He reaches his hand in and pulls out some crumbles. "Try it." He offers me miniature shapes in unnatural colors. "Ignore the cereal and just pick out the marshmallows. You'll see. They're crunchy, but they don't grate on your gums." He

91

gives me a big smile. "Freak show?" He points to himself.

"Gimme the box. I'm not going to eat out of your hand—literally or figuratively," I say, for his benefit and mine. "Is this your room?"

Hanks nods. The space is exactly the right size for a nursery. In Cat's house, that's what the room is for, a toddler or baby. The twin bed takes up one entire wall, and the few feet that are left contain a bedside table on which CDs are stacked, and another wall of built-ins are filled—entirely—with CDs. I pluck out a diamond marshmallow and then a clover, munching them. "Good thing you don't like music."

"I do like music." Hank points to the wall.

"I was kidding."

"It's good, right? Without the cereal part?"

I nod. "Yeah, only, what do you do with the leftovers?"

"Feed them to the turtle." Hank gestures to another room, and I gesture with my full hand of marshmallow-empty cereal, and we leave the world of music.

"Is this Chase's room? I never would have thought Chase would have a turtle. He doesn't seem like . . . like the pet kind of guy."

Hank opens the door to Chase's room. "He's not. Turtle is mine. Pets are, um, important. Having the turtle was supposed to teach me . . ." He stops. "I just don't have space for it in my room, so Chase lets me keep it here. Besides, he's away most of the year now." Hank lifts the mesh top of the turtle's glass cage and chucks the leftover cereal into it. "Here. Give me yours." I drop mine into his open palm, and our fingers touch lightly. I back away. "Take a seat if you

92

want. Chase's bed is bigger than mine anyway."

I'm sure it is, I think when I see evidence of Chase's player-boy mentality. A sign over the bed reads, LINE FORMS HERE with an arrow pointing down. The bottom part of the walls is wood-paneled in here too, but the top half is dark green, and unlike the blank walls in Hank's room, they are dotted with old posters and faux military signs. All the debris of eighth grade and high school. Hank stands underneath a poster of a girl splayed on top of a red corvette, her cleavage threatening to break out of her black tube top. "You like Chase's room?" He watches my eyes scan the walls.

"Nice sign," I say with extreme sarcasm. I read aloud from the sign on the green wall. "'No one admitted without prior written approval of the manager.'" Underneath the word "manager" is a small photo of Chase.

"He lets me in without that," Hank sighs. "It is a cool room, though, I guess."

It doesn't seem that cool to me, all the outdated sports glory—players who have long since retired—and girl booty on display. Hank allows us to sit in silence as he flicks the tin sign on the open bedroom door that reads ENTER AT YOUR OWN RISK. "How come your room's so bare?"

He takes a few steps closer to me. "Because I like it like that. Open air and music."

"Yeah, but why?" Maybe he needs to balance the clutter downstairs or the stuff in his head with his own tiny space. Maybe his musical inspiration and deep poetic soul depend on a lack of girly calendars and eschew bands that people end up liking for five minutes.

Hank plops down on the double bed. Not next to me, exactly, but near. He shrugs. "It's better than this, I guess." He uses his elbow to gesture to the signs and posters.

Hank works the chords of some song I can't name, and I wish he'd tell me which one. That he'd tell me each time his brain flicks to another tune, and how his fingers know to respond.

"Maybe it's an older-brother thing," I say, thinking of other older brothers I've hung out with, and their rooms, the smell of sheets that need washing, the feel of an unmade bed.

Hank sighs. "Or just a Chase thing. You'd see what I mean if you had one."

"I don't have a Chase," I say with my eyebrows raised and a half-smile. I laugh.

"No—I meant an older brother. Or a Chase."

Words catch in my throat. Explanations, too.

"An older brother. But you don't." Hank stares right at me.

"No," I say, and it's the truth. Now's not the time to go into it. Or maybe it's never the right time.

"You're lucky you're an only child." Then Hank looks sorry he said it. "Actually, I take that back. I really take it back." He wipes his palms on his legs. "Chase is . . . important."

I swallow and stare at the wood paneling on the wall. The paneling has fake knots woven into it, making it look sadder than it already is. Let a room look like a room and leave the woods outside where it belongs. "I had one," I tell him.

"One what?"

I sigh and inch forward to the bed's edge, so my feet are resting on the floor. "I wasn't an only child." Hank pauses to do what is really very simple math. His face is blank. I go on. "She was older than me, like Chase is to you, but even older. She was seven and I was three."

"And she died?" Hank's mouth is a straight line, not happy, not sad, something undefined and in between.

I nod. My breath is fast but I have no tears. "It's okay," I tell him. "You can be all upset for me and say how awful it is. Usually people gasp and most even get watery eyes." I grimace. "Dead children, dead siblings, it's all horrific."

But Hank just shrugs. "Is it sad for you?" His voice is placid, monotone, not entirely dissimilar from when I've heard my mother give advice on the phone to parents who are worried their kids are doing drugs or are anorexic or generally falling apart. She is kind but distant.

"No," I say softly, and then for the first time ever, loudly. "No. It's not sad. That's the thing. I don't even remember her, really. Jenny. That was her name." I look at Hank and cut him off at the pass. "I know, okay? There's like a million catchy songs with her name in it. Believe me, I know. Every time they come on the radio, my parents flinch. But I don't. Do you have songs like that?"

Hank thinks. "Everyone probably has a song like that." He breathes in deeply. "'Jennifer oh Jenny.' 'Jenny Say You'll Be Mine.'" Then he picks at the fray on the pocket of his jeans, not chording for once.

"So you're not all sorry for me?" The relief laps at my toes, creeps up my calves, and washes over me. There is nothing worse than not feeling the same thing as someone else. So when you open up and say something that makes them sad but makes you nothing, it sucks.

Hank scoots closer to me until we are side by side on the bed, our thighs just an inch away from touching. He hasn't even tried to hug me to comfort me, which is a good thing on two accounts. "Well, I am sorry for you because"—he looks at Chase's wall—"even though Chase isn't perfect, he's still . . . here."

"They knew she was going to die anyway. My parents. She had this neurodegenerative disorder. . . ." The smallest fragment of despair pokes into my chest. I poke at my tattoo, push the pad of my thumb into the planets. "Well, I didn't even know her, so . . ."

Hank goes on. "'Jenny Don't Be Hasty,' 'Jen My Friend.' '867-5309/Jenny.'" He lets his leg go slack so it touches mine. He turns his head so we're looking at each other in this really weird way from the side of our faces. "Lots of Jennies but no Lianas."

Footsteps in the hall make me jump up off the bed like we've been caught doing something. "Nope. No Lianas."

"Hey, bud." Chase swipes his hand through his surfer locks and waves to Hank from the doorway.

"Hi." Hank stands up and flips his hand back in a wave. "We were feeding Lyle."

Chase grins at us. "Lyle digs his Charms, man. Gotta give him that." We stand there for a few seconds, us and the turtle and Chase, the box of Lucky Charms bright red against the green walls.

"I should go," I announce. "Got to get to the lab early tomorrow. Planets and stars are waiting."

Hank nods and scuffs out the door wordlessly, past Chase. I make to the doorway, right near the sign. Chase's eyes scan me from toe to top, stopping right at my mouth.

"Chase has planets and stars on his ceiling," Hank says from the hallway, and lopes off downstairs.

I'll bet he does, I think about saying, but reel it in. I've said enough for one night. "Bye," I say to Chase before I go.

"Maybe you'll see them sometime," Chase says. He's in his room now. He looks at me but doesn't meet my gaze. "See the sign?" He points to where I'm standing, at the sign behind my head. "'Enter at your own risk,' right?"

CHAPTER 10
HANK

Liana leaves, and I feel horribly disappointed.
And not because I didn't kiss her. Well, yes, okay, partially
because I didn't kiss her. I know nothing about girls, but I
have seen enough movies to know that sitting on a bed thigh
to thigh is the kind of situation that often leads to kissing.

Chase makes me feel stupid too, when he passes by my
room later. "Dude," he says. "Your girlfriend has a killer
rack. You've gotta hit that."

I don't know how to respond to this. I kind of want to
tell him that while I've certainly noticed the killer rack, it's
ridiculous to sum Liana up as a body part. I kind of want to
tell him that the use of "hit that" as a euphemism for inter-
course seems creepily violent to me. Most of all, though, I
want to punch him in the face for talking about Liana like
that, for looking at Liana like that.

But that wouldn't end well. It never has in the past.

Instead I just say, "Thanks, Chase."

He stops for a moment and says, "Dude, seriously. I'm proud of you."

And suddenly I don't want to punch him in the face anymore. I kind of want to hug him. But that wouldn't go over well either. "Thank you. Really," I say.

"All right," he says. Just then the phone on his hip buzzes. He flips it open, rolls his eyes, frantically thumbs the keys for a few seconds, and replaces it. "One good thing about your weird stone-age thing with the phone is that she can't hassle you with a hundred text messages a day. God, did I ever make a mistake with Patti. I mean, I thought, you know, naughty nurse, right? I mean, I'm a guy, right?"

I'm not really following. I've started thinking about music, but I know Chase has just asked me if he's a guy. "Right," I say.

"But God, it's like she stalks me twenty-four/seven with this thing."

"Mmm," I say. It's important to develop a few stock responses to pull out in conversations where you're not paying attention, or it would be awkward to tell the truth. I'm a big fan of "Mmm."

"Well, see ya," he says, and he's off to wherever he goes.

And I'm left alone in my room wondering not only why I didn't kiss her, but also why I didn't tell her. She shared two confidences with me. Does this mean I owe her at least one in return? This is where I wish I had the rule book. It occurs to me that in semi-romantic situations, or whatever, there may be rules that don't apply to normal conversational situations. I feel lost. I know that in normal conversations, words are working on two levels, but I can only follow one. Now I feel like there may be at least one more level, making me two levels behind.

There are so many things I don't understand. Like why she is so upset that somebody called her a slut. They didn't even do it to her face. Here, in no particular order, is a partial list of things I've been called to my face in school: freak, geek, loser, retard, dickwad, gaywad, freakazoid, dipshit, dickweed, shit-for-brains, ass clown, asshat, gaylord, homo . . . I could go on. I've heard less and less of this since the ninth grade, but still. I heard enough to figure out a) that I'm not normal, and b) what people say about you doesn't define you. I've certainly been called variations of homosexual enough times, but I'm not attracted to men at all.

Even still, it was a big deal to her. And she told me. I owe her one.

I suppose I owe her two, since it seemed like a big deal to her that she told me about her dead sister that she doesn't remember. I have learned the stock responses people expect in these situations, but I refuse to use them, because I think so many of them are presumptuous. If you say to someone "That must be so hard for you," or "You must be really sad," it sounds like a command. You must be sad. Well, perhaps they're not. Who am I to tell them they should be sad? I know Allie went over it with me a hundred times: it's not a command, really; whatever the words say, it's just a way of people expressing sympathy. I don't care. I won't do it.

What I will do is tell Liana. I will tell her the next time we have coffee.

I get a sudden pang of terror. The last time we had coffee, she ran out for reasons I still don't understand. Today we didn't have coffee. Does this mean we've changed what had been our standing coffee date?

It occurs to me to ask Chase, but then I don't want him mocking me for how far I am from "hitting that."

It may be time for me to reconsider my position with regards to cell phones. Despite Chase's mockery, I've never really felt the need to own one. Primarily because I don't have anyone to call. I can call in to work from my home phone if I am sick, and I'm beyond the age where I need to call Mother to pick me up from soccer practice or something. Not that I actually play soccer.

But now a cell phone would be handy. It would allow me to call Liana and ask "Are we having coffee tomorrow?" As it stands, I could be sitting alone at Espresso Love. Which is what I always used to do happily. But now it seems intolerable.

The songs don't mention this much. They talk about the way love or infatuation, or whatever it is I feel for Liana, makes you happy, or it makes you sad when you lose it, but they don't really talk much about the way it creates discontent; the way it makes the life you had before seem pathetic in a way you never realized. Someone should write *that* song.

The following day I'm consumed with worry about whether Liana is meeting me or not. Unable to sleep at five a.m., I go to the basement and plug in the Gibson and plug headphones into the amp. I've been thinking about The Smiths a great deal lately, and the Gibson was Johnny Marr's choice when playing live, though of course in the studio he used a variety of instruments and effects.

I boot up the laptop I bought last year from a college student who worked as a lifeguard in the summer. I found her on Craigslist. She seemed to feel I was doing her a favor by paying her fifty dollars for a two-year-old computer.

An hour later I have an MP3 of a serviceable cover of The Smiths' "You Just Haven't Earned It Yet, Baby." I like this song because it allows me to play soft on the verses and hard on the chorus, which I'm hoping will show the people choosing the acts that I have enough range to be interesting. I also like the song because it suggests that suffering is a prerequisite for happiness. I e-mail it to the concert organizers and hope for the best.

I go to work, and hours pass, but I don't really notice anything that happens during them. I ask Stan if I can leave work half an hour early. He tells me to go ahead and make it a full hour. I will have to make up this hour at some point if I'm going to stay on my Jazzmaster money-saving schedule.

But for today it's worth the financial hit to be able to get some peace of mind. I walk over to the lab, where I hope Liana is working. I find a comfortable tree outside and wish I had a guitar with me. Not that I could plug in out here, so I'd have to go with an acoustic guitar anyway, but it would still give me something to do with my hands, with my mind.

I want to pace and run my hands through my hair very

badly, but I'm afraid of looking like freak when she emerges from the lab. If she emerges from the lab. Finally I have to do something, so I close my eyes and picture my Gibson in my hands. I start playing the chords to The Smiths' "Ask," but my brain keeps trying to worry about Liana. So I sing along. Quietly.

And I find that the world goes away, which is a relief. There's nothing but my hands on the (imaginary) guitar and the words coming out of my mouth.

I'm nearly through the song, still singing, when I hear a voice besides my own.

"Hank?" It's Liana. I open my eyes and see her smiling at me. I look down at my hands and get embarrassed. "What are you doing here? Aren't we having coffee?"

"Well, I didn't know if we were or not because last time you had to leave, and then last night we went to the beach and I didn't know which place to meet you, so I figured I'd meet you here. I suppose if I had a cell phone I could have just called you. If I had your number. I'm thinking about buying a cell phone." I'm babbling. She's staring at me. "I'm sorry. The singing, the air guitar—I guess it looks pretty weird."

She smiles. I want to fall into her smile. "It might be weirder if you couldn't sing. You're really good."

"Oh. Thank you. I . . . My MP3 player is on the fritz and—can I ask you something?"

"Sure."

"If I were to get a cell phone, would it be all right if I sent you a message from time to time? I find myself thinking of things I want to tell you during the day, but they're little things, you know, not really enough to hang an entire conversation on. I thought it might be cool if I could just send you something like that—kind of like a *nice* note. Even though it wouldn't be anonymous."

She smiles and laughs. "That kind of note sounds good."

"Oh good, because Nurse Patti texts Chase all the time, and he complains about it a lot. Do you have any idea what kinds of phones are good? What kind do you have?"

"Hank. Do you want to go look at phones instead of having coffee?" Liana stands with her hands facing up.

"Oh. Well, yeah, that would be great. Where do . . . I don't even know where one goes for such a thing."

She smiles at me, twinkly. "One goes to Atlantic Wireless. It's a block from the beach."

"Oh. Cool." We start walking. I'm so relieved that she's here and we're together that I just feel exhausted from all the worrying I did.

I want to tell her. I really do. It's actually all I can think about. Except that she's talking about her project and her work in the lab while I rehearse my speech in my mind, and I guess I'm swinging my arms a lot, which I guess is something I do when I walk.

She's swinging her hands a little bit, and my hand on the backswing catches her hand on the front swing, and suddenly we're holding hands. This has the effect of wiping all the data from the hard drive of my brain.

"I. Um," I say. "I wasn't. I mean." I am trying to tell her that I didn't just bump into her hand as a dishonest, or perhaps underhanded, ha-ha way of holding her hand. I am also not letting her hand go.

"I know. It's totally fine," she says. We don't talk for a block or two, and this time I understand. It's not a failure of conversation. It's just chilling out for a second.

We arrive at Atlantic Wireless. Why are we here again? Oh yeah. The phone. Liana lets my hand drop as we head into the store.

Thirty-five minutes later I emerge with what Liana assures me is a sweet phone. It has a full QWERTY keyboard for ease of text messaging, and with the optional memory card that I opted for, it will hold four hundred songs in MP3 format. Which is a pretty paltry number of songs, but since my other MP3 player has been showing an unhappy face on the screen for the last month or so, it's an upgrade.

The only problem is that it's put me back by more than a few days in my Jazzmaster savings plan. I can no longer afford the Jazzmaster by the end of summer. But if it doesn't sell by the end of summer, I should be able to scrape up enough by late September. Depending on how many hours Stan gives me. Business falls off after the summer people leave.

Liana and I don't hold hands when we get out of the store. I don't know what this means. I'm afraid to ask. We walk down to the beach. Families are starting to pack up for the day, college girls are trying to squeeze the last few bits of melanin out of their skin, and out on the pier, guys with long poles are fishing. I see the spot where the second stage will take place, and I remember something I can say to Liana.

"So I sent in my entry for the music fest today."

"Beachfest? That's so cool. I really can't believe you've never played it before."

"Yeah. I guess I just never . . . I haven't felt really comfortable sharing that part of myself with a lot of people. People from school, you know."

"Mmm," she says, which probably indicates she's not really listening. Is she wondering why we're not holding hands? Is she wondering what the hand-holding implies? Well, she probably knows what it implies. I, however, am at a loss. And I don't want her to think I know what it means, that I've read the signs and am acting accordingly, when I'm just standing there staring at the signs having no idea which way to go.

"So I have Asperger's syndrome," I say.

Liana stops and looks at me. "That doesn't sound good. What is it?"

"It's an autism spectrum disorder. What it means is that I don't . . . What they say is that I have difficulty reading social cues. Like right now, I have no idea how you're reacting to what I'm saying. Whereas someone else might be able to look at your face or your posture or something and understand what this means to you, I have no idea. I know that I don't know, which I guess is helpful, but I still don't know. You know?"

"Uh, not exactly. And if it makes you feel any better, I don't know how I'm reacting to this either." She tucks her hair behind her ears, but the wind doesn't accept that.

"So anyway, Asperger's syndrome is characterized by difficulty with social skills, and also by intense and often narrow interests. Which I guess is what music is for me. It could be worse, I guess—there was a kid in my social skills group who knew everything about public transportation. Routes, schedules, the whole thing. He rode buses for fun. At least I don't ride buses. Oh yeah, I tend to babble. I guess you noticed that. I'm doing it now. I know all these rules, but it's like . . . Do you take Spanish?"

"Yeah."

"So I can have a conversation in Spanish, right, basic *cómo estás* kind of stuff, but I'm constantly thinking about the rules and whether I'm messing it up, and the thing is for me that conversing in English is kind of the same thing. Not that I'm worried about verb tense or anything, but I just have to always be thinking about the way that most people expect a conversation to go and remind myself to do those things. And sometimes when I'm nervous or something, like right now, I forget and just babble, which I guess I'm still doing."

I stop and take a breath. I look at Liana, but not for too long. People find that disconcerting. She stops walking and sits down on the beach. I keep talking. "The thing about the East Coast is that you can't watch the sun set over the ocean. I'll bet that would be cool. I've seen sunrises, of course, over the ocean, but never a sunset. Are you angry at me?"

Liana stares out at the sea. "Oh God, no, Hank. I'm not—" She laughs. "I was going to say 'What would make you think I was angry?' but I guess—"

"Yeah, I'm pretty much flying blind. You just seem different."

She sighs. "I guess I am. Listen, I should get home. My parents have people coming over, and my dad's, like, actually here for a change, so I should go."

"Okay. Are you sure you're not angry?"

"It's one of the only things I'm sure of right now."

"Okay, then," I say. "Bye."

"Bye," she says. I wish I could say I stare out at the sea in contemplation of my romantic longing, but the truth is I look at her butt as she walks away. Finally Liana and her butt are out of sight, and I realize I don't know if I'm going to see her tomorrow. Or, for that matter, ever.

I slide open my phone and send her a text message. *Coffee tomorrow?*

I walk home, and my phone stubbornly refuses to ring. I spend a long time while I'm walking scrolling through menus, making sure I haven't missed her response. Nope. There just hasn't been any. Maybe she's busy making dinner and can't hear her phone.

When I get home, my stomach is churning with worry. I just hope I don't have to see Chase, because he'll tell me that I should never have told her. And then Mother will tell me that a girl who doesn't like me for myself doesn't deserve me anyway, and I will think about how lonely and sad I am, and about how I don't care if somebody deserves me or not. Maybe I will cry. It seems possible.

I open the door quietly and walk up the stairs to my room, skipping the third step where the split wood creaks when you step on it. When I reach the top of the stairs, I see Chase coming out of his room. I silently curse my luck.

"Hey, stud!" Chase says, smiling. I am trying to work up enough energy to smile back when my phone gives a loud beep. I whip it out, open it up, and read the new text message from Liana: *Absolutely. And thank you for telling me.*

Now I don't have to fake my smile. Chase looks at me and looks down at the phone and shakes his head. "That's how it starts, my man. That's how it starts. Now you're on the leash."

He ambles downstairs, and I head into my room and flop onto the bed. Five minutes later, I realize I'm still smiling.

CHAPTER 11
LIANA

My mother's office is all about pamphlets. She stores them at home and carts them to the school guidance office when they run out or if there's a special assembly or something. They are stacked up on the white shelf near her desk. Got herpes? You can read about it here. Need to choose birth control? Grab a leaflet. Friendships getting you down? Boyfriend treating you like dirt? Pressures from parents hurting your psyche? Perhaps you need a pamphlet. I have never read these pamphlets. I have never so much as unfolded one of the cream-colored booklets with bold lettering that reads: *Dating: Am I Ready?* Or *Cutting: Why It Really Hurts.*

From the open window I can smell the burgers on the grill, hear my dad's loud laugh, but not the reason for it. Probably one of Bill Abramson's jokes. One he'd edit if I were down there too. Parents are different when they're around their friends—and with Lauren and Jacob Abramson off at summer journalism school and camp respectively, I feel totally out of place among the parental realm. So much for leaving Hank for a family dinner. I study the pamphlets on offer, still not touching them.

When we were sophomores, Cat once snagged one and did a dramatic reading for me. I still remember her overly concerned dictum: *And if you cannot resolve such issues as these on your own, please do yourself a favor and seek guidance.* That's the main point of all the cream, blue, green, white, yellow, and pink pamphlets—to make you see my mother. She's the guidance counselor at Melville West, where I go, but I don't see her at school except to avoid her in the hallway, or, before I could drive, I'd meet her at her faculty parking space for a ride home. The same is true for her home office. My mother comes in here when she's finished her daily baking regime, but I steer clear of this room because it feels too much like I've done something wrong. Or I'm being judged or something. The pamphlet collection has expanded—Cat would be thrilled. I scan the titles: *Peer Pressure, Drinking: Decide for Yourself, Drugs: Are They Worth It?, Why Am I Alone?, Is My Body Making Decisions for Me?* I swear, whoever has the job of writing this crap could use a tutorial.

Then I see what I came for. With my bare feet on the plush beige carpet, I stand on my tiptoes to reach it.

"Do you need something, Liana?" My mother is at the doorway, her khaki shorts crisp, the collar of her light pink shirt folded down. She sees my reach but doesn't respond to it.

I grab the blue paper and pocket it. "Nope—all set," I say, and wish for just one damn non-closed-off second she'd rush over to me and hug me and smooth my hair and say something like, *Whatever it is that's bothering you we'll solve it. Let me help you.* But she doesn't. Because the framed social work diploma on the wall and the placard on her desk say it all: she is a professional.

I leave the adults to ponder such questions as mustard or mayo, and head to the front steps, where I sit, burger-on-English-muffin in hand, to read what I suspect will elucidate nothing. My eyes read the words but they seem to be skirting around the issues. *Often, communication is difficult. Have you ever tried to get your point across to someone but felt as though your words were not being heard?*

I take a bite of mustard-covered burger, swig at my seltzer water, and try to find something resembling anything worthwhile on the page. Last spring, for extra credit, I wrote essays about particular scientific problems—issues of weight and matter, confluence of electricity in weather patterns, predictions for environmental conditions based on preexisting criteria. Franca Lorenti, the Italian science maven who was at the school for a semester, taught me one important lesson: to properly facilitate scientific discovery and examinations, one mustn't be confounded by too many words. Basically, cut to the chase.

Finally, the back of the pamphlet tells me what I want to know. Everything else was pretty much what Hank had told me on the beach. That he has trouble interpreting gestures or facial expressions, and might move his body oddly. Suddenly the magic of his hands always working chords starts to vanish. His speech—the way it sounds staccato almost, overly thoughtful—isn't so much the product of intense musical passion; it's just a syndrome. People with Asperger's have hampered social skills. As I reread the paragraph, I put Hank in wherever there's another pronoun. Hank has hampered social skills. Hank has a developmental disorder that affects his ability to effectively communicate with others. Hank has an all-absorbing interest in particular topics such as doorknobs, French literature, trains, and Victorian glass. Then I take out the last part and put in music.

My butt feels cold on the stone steps, and my feet are dotted with mosquito bites. All the citronella candles are in the backyard with my parents, and it appears that every single insect that can fly and bite has charged to where I'm sitting. I swat at the air with the pamphlet, my mind retracing all the words, all the versions of Hanks. The earth seems to rupture when you find out something about someone that you never knew. Something huge. And I'd bolted from the beach like I'd bolted from Pren Stevens and Jett Alterman and boys before them, but not for the same reason. I had to get home for dinner, right? And maybe Hank does have these rigid patterns they talk about on the page in my hand. Maybe he does know way too much about who played on what album and which guitar changed the face of rock as we know it, and maybe he'll never be one of those people even if he wants to be.

I clear my soggy paper plate to the sink and take note of

Dad's orange blood-pressure cuff (real name, sphygmoma-nometer) on the kitchen island, front and center yet again. He actually keeps a log of the risings and fallings, charting the systolic and diastolic. When I see the cuff out, I know he'll be home for at least a few days; otherwise he'd keep it near his suitcase. I give a halfhearted glance at his column of numbers and see a big red check—everything's A-OK. Shocker.

My mother finds me on my way upstairs to my room to fin-ish my notes on today's lab work, which I never did because of being with Hank.

"Thanks for dinner, Mom," I tell her. She waits for me to say more, and I contemplate spilling the info about Hank, but I worry she'll get all guidance on me and offer the pam-phlet I already read.

"So this is about your new friend?" she asks, flicking her eyes on the telltale blue paper. She drops her shoulders. "I saw you in town with him the other day, I think." She puts her hands to her lips as though smelling something or maybe wishing she hadn't told me she'd seen me; it's too bizarre to know your parents can find you outside of the house.

"You were spying on me?' I ask, but not angrily.

"I too like to indulge in iced coffee," she explains. "Am I allowed?"

I nod. "I guess."

"Anyway," my mother says, wrapping up our talk with a voice that makes me feel like I'm in one of her sessions at school, "you like this boy?"

My insides twist. *Like.* Like? What a lame word. "Sure." I wonder if she'd rather I'd grabbed the one on drinking or cutting—perhaps those would be preferable for her daughter's "new friend"? "It's just a pamphlet, Mom."

A smile toys with the idea of spreading on her face, but she doesn't let it happen all the way. "You just make sure . . ." she starts. "Just . . . well, you get extra information. The pamphlet is meant to be a launching point. You know, for further discussion? Because sometimes people do try and sum people up with a label, or . . . or they let single words make them—"

I groan, "God, Mom." She raises her hands to ask what, and I give her a perfunctory kiss on her cheek and head upstairs to graph stars. It's like she is incapable of making the leap that maybe I wasn't talking about myself with the pamphlets. That I meant Hank. *His* one-word definition.

Later, I get outside and tilt my head up to the open sky and look at the moon, noting its position in my book, the cluster of stars, the constellations. Hank is so much more than what any pamphlet could say. He has his quirks, his chording ticks, his sky-infinite knowledge of music, but who am I to say that's bad?

I look at my parents' window to see if maybe my mom is checking up on me here, minus the iced coffee. But she's not. I shake my head at her even though she can't see the gesture. Then—right then—I realize my mom sort of had a point. The one-word summing up with "slut" could just as easily replace the one word of "Asperger's." You cannot define

115

someone like that, at least every aspect of them. The feeling swarms over me, giving me chills, making every pore of me know for sure this is true. The note is wrong. Sitting on the porch, I make plots on my graph, careful not to smudge the ink with my left hand. A plane goes by, blinking in the darkness, an object out of place among everything else up there.

The night air is warm, just enough to make me want to linger, and I do, writing more in my notebook: *Stars within a typical galaxy are so far apart that the chances of two colliding are slim to none. But in some dense regions, known as star clusters, they are much more likely to cross paths.*

From my back pocket, my cell phone bleeps and I debate not checking it but then give in.

Looking forward 2 coffee 2morrow.

I find myself reading the text two ways: the way I would have if Hank had never told me about the Asperger's, which is "He's probably half excited for coffee and half trying out his new phone." And the way I will have to reexamine everything now that I know. Because, like it or not, everything is different. Even if I want him to be the same, I've read the pamphlet. And read it late. What if he'd told me right away, way back when he showed up in the bathroom at the hospital? He seemed so cool then, unflappable, unflustered. But with the pamphlet on my desk, that scene is changed: he's semi-unhinged. Not really aware of his environment so he bursts in where he shouldn't be.

Just like maybe he shouldn't seem all broody and intense at Espresso Love. Just like he isn't edgy on the beach, more nervous. I sit with my knees pulled up under my T-shirt and stare at the text and how to decipher it. I want to say it means something more, that each and every word and gesture from him is now this big cloud of diagnoses, but I only come up with the same thing as if he'd never told me: he's just excited for coffee and is trying out his new phone.

But it isn't totally the same, and I want to shake things up. Isn't that what Hank said? That he should try new things? Or at least that's what Chase said he should do. So instead of analyzing the text any further for cues that Hank himself probably wouldn't even recognize, I text him back. The pamphlet detailed the patterns set up by kids with Asperger's, how routine is important, or needed. But Hank showed up at my lab. He broke the coffee routine we had established. And we went to the beach. And I brought him my mother's vanilla hazelnut brownies at Planet Guitar. So he's capable of fracturing the patterns. Just like I am. *Forget Espresso*, I write. *Forget Planet G. and the lab and all the other places we've been so far. Forget all that faux intensity I was putting on you. Blow off work and meet me at the Arcade at ten a.m.*

A century ago Melville was this seaside escape for people from the big cities. They built big wooden houses with wide porches to rock on, elegant oceanfront hotels, and quaint streets like Ocean Boulevard. Tiny cottages like the one where Hank lives were thrown up in a construction frenzy— places for the average people to spend their summer vacations. Then there were World Wars and Depressions and all the other big events that kind of put a damper on seaside frolicking, and the big hotels got boarded up, and more than one huge wooden house was turned into condos. But then, like everything else in this world, the cycle started over and city people decided Melville was this forgotten treasure, and all the old places—the pier, the beach, Ocean Boulevard, and the Arcade—were lovingly restored. You can see all of this documented in photographs that line the walls of Sweet Nothings, the candy store where Hank and I are choosing which overly sugary confection to start our day with.

"I know you like M&M's," he says, and points to the jar of them. In an effort to recreate the Ye Olde Time feel, the walls are lined with bulbous glass jars, each one filled with bright hard candies or blue chewy dolphins or miniature chocolates dotted with rainbows sprinkles.

"Not in here," I say. "I like them only in the package. It's not that they're different. It's just . . ." I take a plastic bag and scoop a few Swedish Fish into it, then move on to the sour strips, which require finesse with the tongs. "I wouldn't want to waste my penny candy on something so average as M&M's."

Hank does a combination shrug and nod. "I get that." He stands watching me fill my plastic polka-dotted bag while his bag remains empty.

"Don't you want something?" We're the only two people in here, and I'm sure it's not my imagination that he seems different today. Maybe he regrets telling me. Maybe some of his magic has worn off. Sort of like after I kiss someone— all that wondering disperses. I plunge the scooper into the M&M's. "Actually, I changed my mind. I will have some. Here—you want—" I pause the scooper in midair.

Hank starts to chord, but because he's holding the polka-dotted cellophane bag, each movement makes a crinkling noise. He gets so into his chronic gestures that he ends up bumping into me, and a shower of rainbow candies winds up all over the black-and-white tiled floor.

"Hank, come on!" My voice is more annoyed than I want it to be—more annoyed than it should be.

Hank finally emerges from his chording stupor. "Oops. Sorry." He crouches down and starts picking up the M&M's one by one. He looks up at me, and in one instant I can feel myself split —torn between what I'd thought he was, this undiscovered edgy musician, and what he is—this semi-dorky, confused, emotionally awkward boy with pale skin and calloused fingers. He is all those things he said, all those insults and words. And then the other route is this: he is exactly the same person as he was before he even told me. I bend down, and together, plucking each little red, blue, orange, and green circle, we clean up the spillage.

"You know there used to be light brown M&M's?" I tell him.

He nods. "I heard that." He reaches for one of the remaining yellows.

On purpose, I reach for the same one and let the side of my hand touch his. "I bet they tasted better, you know? Even though all of these taste the same, really."

Hank nods as though I've said something incredibly profound. "Maybe they'll reintroduce them."

I stand up and yank him up by the hand. "Like a retro pack?"

"Yeah, like that. Like a greatest hits album. All the old phased-out candies and crayon colors." He eyes my bag of treats. "You're stacked—" He blushes and then allows himself to crack up.

I look first at my shirt—another cast-off from my parents' old stash in the basement. This time a Reggae Fest '87. "That I am. However, I am also *stocked*—" I display my bag of goodies. "Which is what I believe you meant to say."

Hank hurriedly shoves a mélange of chocolate-covered whatevers and sour somethings into his bag, snags mine, plops them both on the scale by the cash register, and pays the clueless freshman whose head is buried in a gossip magazine. Before I can thank him, we're out of Sweet Nothings, standing in the morning sun. The air is clean and still, with just enough chill to make everything feel clear, normal. I want to tell Hank that it's okay. That even though it's messy, that what he told me is—

"You're thinking about it, aren't you?" Hank hoists himself up on the metal rails that border the pedestrian-only area. "I can tell because you're quieter than normal. Allie says that means people are thinking—and not necessarily good or bad. But you usually look right at me, and today you're looking everywhere but."

I stare at the Sweet Nothings sign: bubble letters outlined in pink, dotted with different colors to make it appear that a baker has sprinkled it. James Frenti kissed me right there, in broad daylight last year, and I remember thinking beforehand—because I knew he would—that if we went on to be a couple, a real couple that kissed all the time and told each other things and walked around town together with our hands clasped—that we'd have this sweet thing—this sugary, lively place where we had our first kiss.

"Now I'm looking at you," I tell him, and make sure my eyes don't leave his. "But yeah, I was thinking about it." I keep focused on him but walk toward him, my hand gripping the cellophane bag.

"Now you probably want to run. I get it." His face doesn't look bothered by what he said or assumed, but his eyes do; not like he's crying, but like he could if he thought about it.

I glance over my shoulder at Sweet Nothings, at the littered kiss I remember, and then I keep walking so my stomach bumps into Hank's knees where he's perched on the railing. "I already did that," I tell him. And then I clarify. "Ran away, I mean. It's like, what I do."

"So you're going to do what you don't do?"

I untwist my candy bag and wave a blue dolphin in his face. "Something like that." I wait for him to speak. In the meantime, I decapitate the aquatic mammal.

"God, remind me never to piss you off." Hank's eyebrows are raised, his eyes back to normal, all sea-glass green and bright. He laughs and studies his own bag of candy. "I don't even know what I shoved in here."

I peer at it. "Looks like you betrayed common candy sense and got a fair bunch of Licorice Allsorts. Gross."

Hank hops down from the railing, landing with a thud on the pavement next to a pot of brightly colored flowers. The Melville Community Association spends part of each spring beautifying the boardwalk area to entice summer residents to keep funneling money here, so I say, "Careful not to disturb the pansies," and then I realize they're actually marigolds.

Hank hums a tune. "Marigolds always make me think of 'Jennifer Juniper'—Donovan, 1968. You know it?" I shake my head. He sings a little for me.

"Your voice is really . . ." I start, but Hank's looking up the boardwalk.

"It's about Jennifer Boyd. Pattie Boyd's sister. Pattie was married to George Harrison. And then Eric Clapton. But Jennifer Juniper has this quality to it . . ." Hank keeps looking up the boardwalk and begins walking away from Sweet Nothings.

"Another Jenny song," I say.

"No," he corrects, glossing over the reference to my sister. "Jennifer. Is that what your parents called her?"

I shrug. The truth is, I don't even know. "Hank?" I chew my dolphin, wishing I had somewhere to spit it out because it's got a minty flavor I can't stand. "This dolphin is gross."

Hank swivels, turning his attention back to me. "All I can offer you is licorice."

"Now that sounds like a sad song." I grin at Hank and he grins back, so I sing the words to him. "All I can offer you is licorice."

"Too bad you had to be . . . such a bitch," Hank sings to me.

I let my eyes go wide and put my hand to my mouth in faux shock-horror. "And all because I couldn't tolerate your licorice . . ." I sing, but before I complete the lyric, Hank interrupts with:

"Hey! Chase! Wait up!" Hank rifles through his candy and picks out a plain chocolate Kiss. "Here. This'll take away the bad taste." He nudges me forward with his elbow, and we walk together toward his brother, who's milling around the town flagpole with a group of guys I don't know.

Chase gives Hank the what's-up reverse nod with his chin, and Hank introduces me as his friend Liana Planet. Plan-it.

"Pluh-net," I automatically correct. Hank retries the name but ends up saying planet all over again, but in a way that's comforting to me. One of Chase's friends says my name the real way just to make a point, but before they can actually harass Hank, Chase steps in and eyes me like we're at some keg party.

"No intros necessary," Chase says, and then, his shaggy surfer blond hair collecting each and every sun ray, adds, "We're slumming in the Snark—want to join?"

Photos of the Arcade date back to the glory days of Melville Beach—all cotton candy, ring tosses, and women in bonnets. Even though it's redone now, the Arcade is more commonly referred to by locals (at least local kids) as the Snarkade, because it's pretty crappy. And yet we still go there, but mainly as an ironic gesture. The way the goths at school hulk together at the swing set in town at night.

"Check it out—I'm a Skee-Ball champ!" Chase bellows when we're inside the cool dark. The Arcade's shaped like a ballooning tent even though it's shingled, and inside is a street map of old pinball games, Skee-Ball, and Air-Hockey.

Hank pulls me aside. "We don't have to stay if you don't

want to." He leans in to my ear, each word nestling in on the next. I keep my head right where it is and nod. "But I have lots of nickels." He pats his leg, to the very noticeable bulge in his pocket that of course isn't what I thought at all, and shows me the bag of change as evidence. "If you run out of guitar picks, nickels are a pretty good substitute." He air strums.

"I'm just glad it's a bag of coins." I laugh, leaving the second part innuendo.

Unsaid, that is, until Hank says it. "You mean, not a boner."

I blush like it's the first time I've ever heard the word. Which it isn't. "Yeah, Hank, because of that."

"Hey, Strummer Boy, come on and show yer stuff!" Chase waves us over. "And while you're at it, sling some of that change my way, will you?" Chase is overanimated and swaying just enough to make me wonder what he put in his morning coffee.

"What'd you put in your coffee this morning?" I ask, taking Hank's cue to say what's on my mind.

Chase flings a Skee-Ball into a pocket, gaining eighty points and a tongue-length of tickets. "Wouldn't you like to know," he answers, but doesn't look at me. He has a way of speaking to me that makes me feel like I could be anyone. Anybody.

"Kahlúa?" Hank guesses, and after pumping in a handful of nickels, sets us both up for a game. We take turns swinging our arms, sending the balls into the air, trying for the top score, until a pile of tickets collects on the ground and Chase has gone through half of Hank's coin stash, and his buddies, clustered by the Air-Hockey, come to observe our three-way contest. Except that I suck, so it's not really a contest.

Hank is steely-eyed, determined, and he and Chase begin to outlap me, so I pretty much drop out and watch them. Miller, Brian, Derek, Marty, all the guys Chase has clustered around him are decent-looking, in a catalogue way, and being this close to them makes me wish just for a second that I could drop my experiment and get back to one of the things I like even more than candy: kissing. As if on cue, one of the guys puts a palm on my shoulder, supposedly to peer in closer to the game, but not. I wriggle away, scooting closer to Hank. It occurs to me only then, once I pick up Hank's dropped bag of penny candy, that my first instinct was to kiss some random college guy and not to kiss Hank. I look at the ground and wonder why that is, wonder how many flip-flopped and sandaled feet have stood right here, watching and playing games.

Hank mouths the words to the song playing on the scratchy speakers overhead, and when the lyric says, *Joker, smoker, Midnight toker*, Chase's buddy points to him and says, "Dude, this is about you."

"Screw you, Marty." Chase has a ball in each hand, double-timing them into the baskets.

Hank whips a ball into the smallest pocket, gaining in this round, and Chase flips his head back in competitive spirit and turns to his friends. "Wanna see me win?" They clap and laugh, sending enough breath my way to solidify my guess: they have been drinking—either way into the late hours last night, or way way too early this morning. So much for college maturity.

"Hank's going to win," I say, and point to his score. Hank looks at me from the side, just a flick of his eyes, and stops singing along enough to let me know he's grateful.

Chase stops in midswing, displaying the small brown ball as though he's on a game show, and then, with two wide strides, climbs up the entire Skee-Ball game and plunks it into the 100 point section. "Reigning champion!" he announces from the top of the game. His cronies clap, and it's such a lame pose that Hank laughs a little, and I do mostly in a cringe-worthy way. Hot and hammered, Chase doesn't exactly advertise intellect. "I rule!" Only then, on his way down from cheating, his knee buckles. 'Uw—shit!" He adds to this with a bunch of curses and grimaces while Hank and another guy help him down. "I'm fine," Chase says when he's back standing on the floor. He shrugs off the help. "I'm fine."

Hank goes back to flinging balls into the tiny circles, desperate to beat Chase's score, and I stand there half paying attention until I see one of those old fortune-telling machines. Complete with a bearded, turbaned guy and a crystal ball that is sadly made of wood and flaking white paint, the game is a relic of times gone by. Or maybe people always want to know what will happen. I slide a nickel into the slot and then realize it takes four. I pat my pockets for extra change but find none. Before I can raid Hank's stash, Chase appears behind me, or maybe he was there already, I can't say for sure.

"So, what lies ahead?" His breath is warm on my neck.

Feeling how close he is to me, I don't turn around. I shrug as a response.

"Come on, at least tell me my fortune."

"I'm not omniscient," I tell him. He takes my left hand, pries it open from its clenched position, and presses a quarter into it.

"Go ahead. See what the magic man has to say." He leans into me, placing a hand on my hip. If it were night, or we were alone, or it was last year, or even two months ago, I know what I would do. So easy to turn around, be inches from his face, see that look, both of us acknowledging what we want to do.

I focus on the peeling paint, the fortunes that never come true, the fake beliefs we all have in being told what's going to be rather than what is right now.

"It only takes nickels," I spit out, my voice harsh. I move away from him.

"Well then, I guess my quarter won't help." Chase grins at me, and for just a second, our eyes meet. "You gonna pay me back or what?"

Later, when we've left the Snarkade, and Chase's pack has gone home to debuzz, Hank and I walk the length of the boardwalk all the way from town up past the pastel-painted stately homes, past the row of stores, past Ocean Boulevard and the tiny cottages like the one where Hank lives, all the way to the Landing, where there's a kid-sized merry-go-round and a really pathetic planetarium.

"Which do you want to go to?" Hank sticks his arms out like the Scarecrow.

"Well, I'm pretty sure I won't fit on one of those horses." I glance to where a little girl waits for the music to begin so she can have her carousel ride. "So I guess it's the worst planetarium ever."

"The WPE," Hank confirms, and swings his bag of candy toward the entrance. I can't tell if he saw Chase and me at the fortune-teller. If he cares. If he would even understand what it meant.

But we don't go in. Instead, Hank pulls me around the back of the building, to the fire escape. "Hold this," he says, and with one foot on the brick wall, jumps up high enough to pull down the metal ladder. "Climb up. Ladies first." Then he gives a wry smile. "No one really uses the word *lady*, do they?"

I don't answer with anything but a laugh and an odd feeling of guilt about what could have happened with his brother. I grip my candy stash in my mouth so I can climb up. We go all the way to the top, wedging ourselves near the WPE's domed window. The ocean is right in front of us, all blue-green and shining, but far enough that we can't hear any crashing waves. What we can hear is the poor-quality narration from inside: "Jupiter is the fifth planet from the sun. It is the fourth brightest object in the sky."

Hank, crunching a piece of rock candy, turns to me. "What are the other ones?"

He can't have seen us. Surely he would ask about it. "The sun, the moon, and Venus," I say matter-of-factly. I pick through my bag and pull out a piece of red licorice. "Now see, red is fine. And chocolate. But black licorice . . ."

Hank remembers the tune from before. ". . . is a bitch."

"Makes you want to ditch . . ."

The narration, its warbly music and sad old words, sounds again, "Gas planets do not have solid surfaces."

I interrupt. "Their gaseous material just gets denser with depth, blah blah blah."

The music continues. Inside, the star canvas must be shifting, and I can imagine the only three types of people who come here: old people, little kids with their parents hoping to pass the morning, teenagers pawing each other in the darkness. Hank and I are none of those things. "Mars is sometimes called the Red Planet."

"The Red Planet." Hank mimics the sound, his voice low and dramatic instead of monotone like it often is. "Not a bad album name."

"Yeah—maybe you'll use that at Beachfest," I say. I hand him a Skittle because he mentioned he likes the purple ones best.

Hank shakes his head. "No, it's not a real song. I'm thinking more like a cover of Sly & the Family Stone, but really stripped down, and acoustic. Or something. I need some time to work it out. Maybe 'We Can Work It Out,' but it's too done. Too covered. You can't cover a covered song. Unless you're being multilayered, and that's not something I'm really great with."

He isn't great with multilayered and that's why even if he had seen Chase pressed up against me, witnessed Chase breathing into my ear, he wouldn't have gotten the under-tones.

"You'll find it," I say. "The right song." I pause and bite my lip. "Maybe, do you want to come to my house sometime? My parents, they have all these records—and . . . I don't know—I don't really listen to them. But this shirt, it's from their old boxes. . . ."

"Sure," Hank nods. "Yeah." We lean back onto the stucco wall, and the points jab my back, but I don't move because I like being here with him, away from the Snarkade, away from old kisses, away from groups to which we don't really belong—at least not yet. "So what planet are you?" I ask him, and don't really know what I'm saying. Maybe what I mean is, What guy are you, or What will I know about you—as much as I know about Venus?

"Well . . . not the red one," he says. "And probably not the blue one. There's a blue one, that I know." He looks at me, and for just one second I think this is it—my experiment is well and truly over—Hank and I are going to kiss. Right here, on the rooftop, with the ocean as our witness, and the sounds of planets nearby. But we don't. He doesn't. I don't. "I think I'm the rockin'-est planet." Hank cracks up as he says it, and I laugh hard too. "I'm the planet no one has seen, the brightest one that's ever been. The one that can't fake the scene." He sing-raps, and I keep laughing, the kind of laugh that keeps coming out because it's such a weird and not-true thing to say. So not true, that it's true, maybe.

CHAPTER 12
HANK

Mother would probably say I'm out of sorts.
I spent the morning with Liana, which of course was nice,
or better than nice. Stan was more than happy to give
me the day off unexpectedly—I suppose I am a very reliable
employee otherwise, and when I told him that I was going
to meet a girl, there was a moment of silence before he said,
"All right! Go get 'em, Tiger!"

But now I am one day further away from the Jazzmaster. It appears that I may have to choose between the girl
I love and the guitar I love. Not that I love Liana. I don't
think. I don't really know what romantic love is. I know
how I love Mother, and even Chase, and I know that the
way I feel about Liana is different from that, but whether
it's love or not I have no idea. Fortunately, there are enough
songs about this— "Why Can't This Be Love," "Is This Love

That I'm Feeling", and of course "Is That Love" by Squeeze, the band that always reminds me of Liana's breasts, not that they are really ever that far from my mind—that I know I'm not alone in my confusion.

In any case, I now find myself with the late afternoon and early evening to myself. Since this is normally Liana time, I don't know exactly what to do. I try to practice my song for Beachfest, but it just doesn't feel quite right. I look for an excuse to send Liana a text message, but I really don't know what to say. *I am bored and lonely?*

Fortunately, Chase comes to my rescue by staggering down the hall from his room and vomiting copiously into the toilet at four p.m.

Chase just woke up and vomited, I send to Liana. I imagine her reading it and smiling. This makes me think about her mouth. This brings me to my masturbation dilemma.

I recognize this as an irrational fear, but I am afraid if I masturbate while thinking of Liana, she'll know instantly by looking at me. I imagine most people have a way of hiding this information, and I don't have access to that technique, and she'll see my face and think I'm creepy and run away. Which is what most girls do to me, and what Liana does to most guys. According to her.

Similarly, if I masturbate while thinking of someone else— someone, for example from Chase's rather extensive collection of pornography—I think this will feel like a betrayal; Liana will see on my face that I'm attracted to someone else, even some shiny fantasy woman with a tramp stamp from the Internet, and she'll run away. Which is what she does. According to her.

It is fair to say that there's pressure building up that I don't know how to relieve. I am hoping a nocturnal emission may solve my problem.

Not surprised. He was 'faced this a.m. my phone tells me, and I just want to call her to say *Hey, wasn't that fun today, I can't wait to see you again,* but I am reminded of Chase's annoyance at being stalked twenty-four/seven with the cellular phone, and I decide I have to wait at least thirty minutes before I communicate with her again.

Chase emerges from the bathroom. He smells of Scope rather than vomit, but he is otherwise disheveled—his eyes are red, his cheeks are stubbly, he has a rather vicious case of bed head, and he walks with a shambling gait, like a zombie in an old movie.

"I drank way too much. I will never ever do it again," Chase says.

"'Not until the next time,'" I say, completing the line from The Smiths song. Chase punches me in the arm. It hurts, but it's the kind of thing one must brush off if one has brothers. Or so I've been told.

"Shut the hell up," he says. "Don't be a dick to me just because your hot girlfriend keeps blue-balling you." With that he shuffles back to his room and closes the door.

I want to tell him that he's completely mischaracterized our relationship. While it's true that I have occasionally come home from hanging out with Liana with a painful ache in my testicles (one that could, a little online research revealed, be cured by masturbation, but that brings us back to the problem), it's certainly not something she is doing to me intentionally, as Chase implies. It's my problem, not hers. But I think this is a difference in how Chase and I view girls. It's clear that he views his dealings with girls as a nearly commercial exchange. He pays a certain amount of attention and text messages, and he receives sexual contact in return.

I don't understand this point of view, and I don't know which of us is the one who is normal with respect to this issue. Certainly enough girls seem to respond to Chase's "magic" that perhaps his view, odd as it seems to me, is actually the normal one.

And it does occur to me that I may be putting my nascent relationship, friendship, friendship without benefits, whatever it is that Liana and I have, at risk by not "making a move." Again, this is something girls seem to expect. The boy is supposed to assume the risk of moving the relationship beyond the friendship stage. I don't know why this is. But I suppose now that Liana knows about my condition, my *wonderful difference*, as some of the Asperger's blogs would have it, I might be able to fall back on that as an excuse—I can't read social cues, remember; that's why I thought I could kiss you. I suppose it's not an excuse if it's true.

I guess I run the risk of her not wanting to hang out with me anymore, which would be awful and horrible. But it would be more horrible to hang out with her and have her tell me she's going out with someone else.

Fine. I will kiss her. The next time I see her, I will make a move. I do not know exactly how one does this, but I will get it done. I will make clear that I want to "take the relation-ship to the next level."

I am essentially alone in the house. I am thinking about kissing my girlfriend, or the girl who is my friend. It will be tomorrow before I see her again, so hopefully I will be able to find a way to disguise the look on my face by then. After all, how can I do it correctly if I can't even imagine it correctly? I head into my room, lock the door, and emerge two minutes later feeling far more relaxed than I've felt in days.

Mother comes home only a few minutes later. This sur-prises me, as her shift at the post office sorting station ends at five, but she normally works at least two hours of overtime.

"Hey, buddy," she says. "How are you?"

"I am out of sorts," I say. "It's quite unusual for you to be home this early."

Mother smiles. "And that's why you're out of sorts?"

"No. I am out of sorts for other reasons."

"Glad to hear it," she says, flopping into a chair and flipping off her shoes. "I just had to get out of there. One more trip across that floor and I think I would have gone completely insane. I mean, God knows we need the money, but at a certain point, the overtime just stops being worth it. You know?"

"No. I've never gotten any overtime, because even in the summer I don't work more than thirty-five hours a week. Stan's quite clear that he would like to give me more hours, but—"

"Okay, okay," Mother says. "Listen, it's the beginning of my weekend, and I want a margarita. You feel like going to El Mariachi?"

"Yes I do. I enjoy the guacamole-preparation ritual." At El Mariachi, the guacamole is prepared tableside in a stone mortar, with all the ingredients added in the same order every time. I find it very satisfying.

"I know you do," Mother says, smiling. "But listen, no asking the band if they know any *narcocorridos* this time."

I had been reading about a popular Mexican genre of music that chronicles the lives of drug dealers, and figuring the band at El Mariachi would be experts, I asked them about it. They grew surly, and Mother was embarrassed.

"All right."

"In fact, no talking to the band at all," Mother says. She goes to her room, changes her clothes, knocks on Chase's door to ask if he'd like to go to El Mariachi, and receives a string of expletives for her trouble. "Talk about out of sorts," Mother says.

"He vomited at four o'clock," I say. "We saw him this morning, and he was apostrophe faced."

Mother looks at me for a long time as she collects her keys from the table. "There is so much I have to untangle from that little statement," she says. "Get in the car."

I obey, and Mother drives us to El Mariachi.

I explain, in this order, the fact that Chase was intoxicated in the a.m., who I meant by "we," why I wasn't at work, and where I heard someone called apostrophe faced.

At the restaurant, we are seated by the hostess, who is Shelley from school. I had a math class with her in ninth grade. She's dressed in the El Mariachi uniform of Mexican peasant blouse and black skirt, and it is with great effort that I don't stare at her bare, tanned shoulders. If Shelley recognizes me, she gives no indication. She quickly goes from our table over to a table occupied by David Olson, lacrosse-playing star. David is dining alone, and Shelley sits at his table for a moment. It occurs to me that they might be going out. Perhaps he sits here waiting for her shift to end, subsisting on chips and salsa and whatever crumbs of conversation Shelley is able to dole out when her manager is not looking.

"Hank. You're staring," Mother says to me, and I turn back to her. "So I have a couple more questions."

By the time I've finished answering all of Mother's follow-up questions and have covered Liana's interest in astronomy, her dead sister, and her coffee preferences, we are into our second basket of tortilla chips, and Mother is debating whether to order more guacamole. "I feel bad," Mother says. "I just—I don't feel like I can turn down the overtime, you know? The house needs work, and . . . but I'm obviously missing out on a lot. Let's have her over. Tomorrow. Can we? I mean, would that be okay with you? I'd really like to meet her."

"It is okay with me," I say. I whip out my phone and text *Mother invites you to dinner at our house tomorrow. RSVP.* I am happy because now I have an excuse to call Liana when we get home and also because I will get to kiss her at night, perhaps as I walk her home from my house, which seems far more suitable than some daylight kiss outside Espresso Love or on the beach in full view of dozens of students from our high schools.

CHAPTER 13
LIANA

The lab is dark and still except for the light over my work table. One of the faucets drips into a steel basin, the *plunk plunk* sound the only thing audible, save for my own nerves. Why didn't I tell him sooner? Beach walks, personal food preferences, lyrics, hours' and days' worth of conversational connection. But no kissing. I should have explained earlier—over coffee, or at his house, anywhere. I mean, what's the point of keeping stuff from people when they're supposed to be your—your what? Friend? Boyfriend? Hi, I have a dead sister. I told him that. Told him about entering Slutsville, but I just can't bring myself to tell him about my summer experiment. I shake my head and focus back on my notes, which I am turning into a paper. A world of extra credit doesn't make the people floating in it make any more sense.

I transcribe from my journal: *All planets are very faint light sources, especially when you compare them to their parent stars. Detecting such faded light sources is not only difficult, but because the parent star is bright, the already dim light gets washed out. That's why there have been so few documented and seen extrasolar planets.*

"What's an extrasolar planet?" my dad asks. He's been standing near me for a good five minutes, but I'm pretending to be engrossed in work so I can take a few minutes to process why he'd show up at the lab, mid-day, unannounced.

"It's a planet beyond the solar system," I say, and close my notebook. The sound echoes. What does it mean that I am old enough now to know things my parents don't? When did they stop being pillars of information, supreme beings who contain infinite wisdom?

In the background I hear the *plunk plunk* of water dripping, but I try to tune it out. I bet Hank wouldn't be able to let go of the noise and we'd have to run around testing each sink to find the leaky culprit. We'd have one of those movie montages where there's a cool song over shots of us running on the beach, or pouncing from one leaky sink to the next, laughing all doubled over, the whole thing culminating in a moment where we splash each other with the dripping sink water and wind up kissing. I should have made it clear to him right away. But how could I when I wasn't sure about it myself?

Hank will bolt, most likely. Or worse, do the guy thing of hanging around enough so he doesn't seem like a total ass who was in it just for the score, but then slowly fade out—a star gone awry. "Why don't people just say what they need to say?" I blurt out, and the expanse of air in the lab makes my words seem too important, especially to my dad, who isn't the person I'm supposed to confront.

"You're right, Li," Dad says, and leans with both palms on the soapstone. "People should express themselves. Information needs to be shared." He sounds like one of his motivational mugs. "That's why I'm here. . . ."

I furrow my brow. "What?"

Dad pushes his fingers through his hair. It's thinning at the top but still there on the sides. "I have to go in for more tests. There's an advanced screening process . . . LDL levels aside, I might have some blockage—"

"Blockage?" I start to laugh. Not big laughs, but the word is funny. *Blockage.* Maybe we all have blockage. I was blocked, Hank, that's why I didn't tell you. Dad purses his lips. The idea that my full-grown alive dad is having yet more psychodrama that requires tests is so annoying I can't help but laugh again.

"It's not exactly a humorous matter." Dad shoots me a look. "How would you like it if I laughed about your health?" I make a rumpled face to show I am sorry, even if his imaginary illnesses are beyond grating. "Fine. So *your* health isn't the topic here, but still—I feel that you have the right to know about what's happening in this family."

I pause, looking at the planets floating above. Dangling from fishing wire, Saturn, Neptune, all of their solar buddies swing free in the lab's open ceiling space. "The Sun's not the only star that planets orbit. Did you know that?" I ask, standing up and collecting my stuff. "No one thinks about the other stars, or the other planets, but they're out there." I sigh and look at my dad. "I'm sorry you have to have more tests." And I *am* sorry about that. But I'm sorrier that something in my father makes him need to probe and test and worry all the time about his body, which is actually fine. But at least he told me. I need to tell Hank. So I say to my dad, since he's here and Hank's not, "How come you always think something's wrong with you?"

I've never asked him anything like that. It sounds insulting, and maybe it is, kind of, even though I really do wonder why. Dad rubs his hands together as though we're by a campfire or anywhere cozy rather than an echoing laboratory. "Something could be," he says softly.

I don't ask more. Maybe he will let the question sink in, brew a while, and have more to say another time. My heart thuds, my whole self knowing I have to tell Hank or I'll explode. Sunsets, music, baked goods, coffees, they're all okay. They are better than okay. They are planet-big and full and leading somewhere, but not to the land of lip-lock.

I jab my dad's ribs with my notebook. "Or it could be something else, right?" He waits for me to go on. "There are all these patterns . . ." I begin but can't finish. Because his pattern, and my pattern, and my mother's baking, and Hank's chording, they're all too connected right now.

"Would you rather not know about the tests?" Dad asks, and holds the heavy door for us both.

"No, I want to know."

I will tell him. I half close my eyes to the intense sunlight.

I'm always disoriented coming out of the lab; it's like time doesn't move in there—only, I know it moves because the sun is lower, Hank's working a long day hocking guitars or sheet music, and right now I realize what I need to do. Right now. No hesitating. "I gotta go to Planet Guitar," I tell my dad.

He looks pale, draws a big breath. I wish his worries didn't get to him so much. "Give me a lift home first, though, okay?" He pauses. "I was going to walk, but I think it'd be better if I got a ride." He takes my arm like a blind person would, a light grip but needy. "You getting an acoustic?"

"No. No. I'm not—I don't play guitar. You know that." My heart pounds. Not because my dad is home from work days early, or because he's having more tests, but because this is it: I will go to Planet Guitar and tell Hank—just get it out in the open before the official meeting-the-mother dinner. Before the lamb chops or salad or burgers and family fun. Before I sit through some solar system show or venture into a dark movie theater or listen to some song that just makes me forget all the parameters of my no-kiss rule and lay one on him. Our lips can't meet, I'll tell him. Maybe there's a song I can think of that will explain it for me. I buckle my seat belt and lean over to open my dad's door.

My dad is a great editor, a grammarian like no other, and back before he began his frequent-flier accruing, he was that English teacher you always wished you had. The kind that students keep in touch with, to whom they dedicate their novels or credit with their future successes. So when I think about how to tell Hank, I run it by my father first, just because he's here. "If you need to tell someone something and you use someone else's words to do it . . ." I start, my mind churning over lyrics—but all I can think of is songs that result in kissing, not ones that avoid it. "Kiss on My List," "I Want Your (Hands on Me)," "These Lips," "Melding Mouths." Not helpful. "Say if you found the perfect words but . . ."

"It's plagiarism," Dad butts in.

"No, but if it's not like an academic assignment—"

"It's still plagiarism." He looks at his hands and then at my face. Even though he's not a teacher anymore, sometimes he still seems that way. I wonder if I still seem slutty, even though I'm not. If you ever get past what you were. Then it hits me that my dad used to be a father of two and then he wasn't. Isn't. If maybe on those medical forms he fills out all the time he has to pause when it says to list the names and ages of your kids. "Liana." Dad says my name and keeps his eyes on mine. I wonder if he looked at my sister this way ever, his eyes probing, his gaze so tender and comforting that I could cry but I wouldn't.

"I just meant a song. Like in the movies, when they sum up a moment by putting a soundtrack to it." I back up out of the parking lot and head toward home.

"When something's important enough, you kind of have to force yourself to say it. Not pass the buck Hallmark-style." He raises his eyebrows. His tone switches to sitcom dad. "Is there something I should know?"

I shake my head deliberately, slowly, looking in my rearview mirror. I can do it myself. Without lyrics. I can bring Hank whatever my mother's got going in the oven. Brownies. Cookies. Doesn't she say that everything can be solved with a good cookie? Where's that pamphlet? I swallow, picturing Hank's face when I blurt it out. I have to pick a good time. A normal time. Now. And I'll take care of it. Because it is important; it's not something that will fade out like a dying planet or passing song. But I'll just say it simply: we cannot kiss.

CHAPTER 14
HANK

I am glad for the distraction of work. It prevents me from obsessing about Liana's visit tonight and the kiss that will follow. Or, I should say, it gives me something else to do while obsessing about Liana's visit tonight and the kiss that will follow.

Of course, Liana has been to my house before, but that was a more informal drop-in kind of thing and did not involve a meal. Due to everyone's schedule, it's rare that we eat dinner together, and I cannot remember the last time we had someone other than me, Chase, or Mother at the table with us. Chase's relationships never last long enough for a girl to merit this kind of treatment. In fact Chase, uncharacteristically awake before ten, both apologized for being mean to me in the hall, and revealed that he had been drinking from late in the evening until early in the morning in order to get over the stress of his breakup with Nurse Patti in the early evening. Apparently she was more than a little upset and began to throw Precious Moments figurines at Chase. "I swear to God, she was aiming for my bad knee. Psycho!"

"That would certainly seem to be a violation of the Hippocratic oath, though I suppose that might just be for doctors," I chime in.

Chase looks at me for a long moment, then says, "Hank, man, I love you, but you're just on a different planet from me." He pauses, grins, and says, "Or, should I say, you're on a different Pluh-net from me."

"Ah," I say, "you've gone after the mother. Interesting choice. Definitely stepping outside of your usual type. And a married woman to boot."

"No, dorkus, I meant—"

"I know, Chase. I was making a joke."

"Well, you can forgive me for not getting it. It's pretty hard to tell with your delivery, you know."

"No," I say. "I don't."

I left him to ponder this and headed in to work. I've just made my first sale of the day, a midline wah-wah pedal, when the door opens and Liana comes in with a plate full of cookies.

"Hey!" I say. "What are you doing here?" I wish I had a mirror so I could check my face. Not that I'd know what to look for, but if I could at least be convinced that I couldn't see any evidence of my masturbatory fantasy, it would be comforting.

"Nice to see you too," she says.

"Oh, yes, it's always nice to see you. I figured that went without saying, but I suppose it doesn't go without saying after all. I just meant that it was surprising to see you. Because you didn't say you were coming." She has not run screaming from me. Apparently my thoughts of yesterday afternoon remain opaque to her. This is a tremendous relief.

"Well, you stalked me at the lab; I figured I should stalk you at the guitar store. Plus I want to see your true love."

Look in a mirror, for God's sake, I want to say, but I don't. Instead I sputter, "I . . . you want to . . . I . . ."

"The Jazzmaster," she says, looking around the store. She studies the east wall, where the new guitars hang, completely ignoring the vintage guitars on the west wall.

"Oh. Right. That. I . . . uh, can I take, I mean, I sort of assume that the cookies are for me because you've brought me delicious baked goods in the past, but I don't want to—"

"Take them. Please. They're oatmeal chocolate chip with cherries. I hate dried fruit."

"I dislike the brown dried fruits. I hate dates, figs, and raisins, but I like apricots and cherries."

"What about dried apples?"

"Light brown. They're okay."

"Okay, but you can't possibly like dried pineapple. Nobody on earth likes that." She tugs at a strand of hair with one hand, then lets it go, then tugs it again. I'm fairly certain this is a social cue.

"I like it, provided it's not covered in sugar. Which it usually is. Those candied cubes of pineapple are disgusting. But the pineapple's natural sweetness—"

"Can I just see the guitar already?" She continues to tug at her hair. It occurs to me that this may be the "I wish he would make a move" signal, but that can't happen until tonight.

"Sure," I say. "And thank you for the cookies." I bite into one, and it's delicious.

"Stan," I call out. "Can I play the Jazzmaster?"

"No way," Stan barks from the rear of the store.

"I'll give you a fresh home-baked cookie!"

"What kind?"

"Oatmeal chocolate chip cherry."

"Make it three of those and you've got a deal." I glance at the plate that surely holds two dozen cookies. I can certainly spare three. I take Stan the cookies, and he peeks out onto the floor. "Hank. My man. I would blow off work for her, too. And," he mumbles, mouth half filled with cookie. "Mmm! She makes amazing cookies. That's a keeper right there."

"Well, her mom made the cookies, but she is certainly a keeper. The daughter, I mean. I mean, well, I assume the mother, in the eyes of her father, would be a keeper, obviously, since they've been together for—"

"Okay. Stop talking to me and go impress her, for God's sake."

"Right. Okay," I say, and turn around to where Liana is looking at a cherry red guitar.

"This isn't it, is it?"

"No, that's a Gibson Flying V. It's got a pretty metal look to it, but I personally am not crazy about the sound. Though of course I suppose it's remarkable that both Bob Mould and Albert King could play the same guitar and get such different—"

"Where's the Jazzmaster?" she asks.

"Albert King plays it with his right arm in the crook of the V." I could not stop myself from saying that part. Though I tried. "Here's the Jazzmaster."

I delicately take it from the wall and plug it in. "I'm thinking about doing this one for Beachfest," I say. "Though of course it'll sound better when I have all the right effects and stuff."

Liana makes that hurry-up-already motion with her hands, and I start playing "Pipeline." And for approximately three minutes, everything falls away. Liana is gone, the rest of the store is gone, the cookies, Stan, everything disappears except for me, six strings, and a really big whammy bar. I mess up a little on the bridge and wince, but I'm able to recover and get through to the end.

When I finish the song, I kind of come back to the world, and Liana is standing there with her mouth hanging open. I'm embarrassed.

"I know. I messed up on the bridge, and I mean, I can hear the bass and drums in my head, so it sounds better to me. I'm thinking of maybe using an old drum machine I—"

"Will you shut up? That was awesome! I knew you played guitar, but I had no idea you could play like that! Hank! You rock!"

I see Stan at the back of the store giving me two thumbs up. "Yeah," I say. "I guess I do, sometimes. Under the right circumstances."

Sadly, Liana can't stay at Planet Guitar all day, so she goes to the lab, I finish a pretty slow day at work, and then I go home to find Mother in full-bustle mode.

I walk in the door, and Mother is yelling to no one in particular, "I mean, this kind of thing drives me crazy. There is a gigantic energy drink can two feet from the recycling bin. I really can't understand the thought process! You got that far, and it was just too much to make it the last two feet? Jesus, guys, we're having a girl over here. Girls notice things. I don't want her to think we live like pigs, even if we actually do."

Mother picks up the can and puts it in the recycling bin. "Actually, Mother, I saw Chase shoot that can, basketball style. It actually hit the rim of the recycling bin. So that's why it's not in the bin."

"Okay, but then neither one of you thinks to pick the damn thing up! I mean, you know, it's not like I don't feel guilty about how much I have to work. You guys have to pile crap up everywhere to remind me what a bad mother I am. I just wish—"

"That you and Nana didn't hate each other so much and that you would be the recipient of some of Nana and Grand-dad's largesse, not just Chase and me?" The tension between Mother and Nana, my father's mother, is obvious even to me. Perhaps this is because it often results in shouting. Also obvious is the fact that we live here in West Melville and Mother feels obligated to work a great deal of overtime, and Nana and Granddad live in a palatial house in East Melville with a private beach. Chase and I used to spend the night there sometimes, but that hasn't happened since 2003.

150

"Hank, Nana and I don't hate each other. We just—she had ideas about who your dad was and what he was going to do, and I was an unacceptable diversion from her plan. But yeah, some largesse would be nice. I mean, if your dad were still here—"

I don't like where this is going. "Liana likes root beer in glass bottles. I am going to walk down to the store and buy a six-pack. Shall I pick up anything else for you while I'm gone?"

"You know, if you could manage to just pick up your socks once in a while, that would be a big help."

"Consider it done, Mother," I say, already out the door before she can start back on her line of conversation.

I grab the root beer, and by the time I return, Mother is obsessing about dinner and no longer obsessing about the state of the house. I, of course, am obsessing about dinner and what comes after. I want nothing more than to pace around the house and tug at my hair, but I force myself to go to the basement and pick up the guitar.

"There's nothing to be afraid of," I tell myself, but I am afraid. I'm afraid of failure, of course, but also of success. Either way, everything changes tonight, and I'm afraid of change. It's uncomfortable.

I hear Ray Davies in my brain saying that he doesn't feel afraid, and I begin playing The Kinks' "Waterloo Sunset." I love the guitar intro, and I love the idea of not feeling afraid. I play the song over and over, and yet I still feel afraid.

Finally, finally, Liana arrives. I open the door. She's holding flowers.

"Hello!" I say. "I must say I've never received flowers before, but I certainly appreciate—"

"They're for your mom, Hank. Flowers for the table. It's polite."

"Oh." She's staring at my hands, which are chording frantically.

"Whatcha playing?" she asks, pointing at my hand and smiling.

"'Waterloo Sunset.' The Kinks. From the album *Something Else by The Kinks*."

"Oh, right. I don't really know that band. But we have it, that album, I mean. In the basement. Along with about six other Kinks albums."

"Wow! Have you ever listened to them?"

"No—they're—let's just say there's a lot of stuff in our basement we don't exactly deal with."

"You know, if you ever wanted to bring them over, I'd be happy to digitize them for you. I mean, I don't know which albums you have. I personally think it's kind of all downhill after *Muswell Hillbillies*, but—"

"Hey."

"Yeah? Fan of *One for the Road*? Many people are, but—"

"Hank."

"Um. Yes?"

"Are we gonna dine on the stoop here, or do I get to come in?"

"Oh, right, of course. You're standing on the doorstep. Mother will be horrified at my rudeness. Or else assume we're making—I, uh, please come in."

Liana comes into the kitchen. I'm glad she's here, but at the same time, I'm horribly uncomfortable. Mother comes rushing over and extends a hand, introduces herself, and tells Liana isn't she sweet for bringing flowers, she didn't have to do that.

"I'm really sorry about the state of the house. You know, since Hank and Chase's dad died, I've had to work a lot, and I don't exactly get the help I need around here, so it's just me part-time trying to keep up with the full-time mess two boys make. Well, you can imagine."

"Your—I had no idea. I'm so sorry." Liana looks at me. She's frowning. I assume this is because she is expressing sympathy.

"Oh. I. Thank you. I just assumed Hank would have told you."

I look at Liana, but she isn't looking at me. She is staring at the flowers she brought, which are sitting on a chair near the door, waiting for Mother to find some water for them.

Mother turns to me. "Hank? Can you help me in the kitchen? Liana, just make yourself at home. I won't keep him long."

"I got root beer," I say. "In glass bottles. Can I bring you one from the kitchen when I'm done helping Mother?"

"Mmm," she says. She's still looking at the flowers.

"I'll take that as a yes," I say, and head into the kitchen.

Mother stands there, hands on hips, and I head to the fridge to grab the root beer.

"Hank, are you trying to . . . Look, I know you don't

153

like to talk about it, but especially when she's shared stuff with you, you can't just keep stuff like that private. Not in a relationship."

"Stuff like what?"

"Cut it out, goddammit. Did you see the look on that girl's face? She looked like she'd been kicked!"

"Well, Mother, I did see the look on her face, but as you should be well aware by now, I have difficulty interpreting such things. There are some helpful books on Asperger's syndrome on the shelf in the living room, if you'd like me to bring you one."

Mother, red-faced, turns to the sink for twenty seconds, then finally turns back around. When she speaks, her voice is quiet and even. "Go out there and talk to her. Tell her dinner will be a few minutes and talk to her and apologize to her and try to fix this."

I've had enough of Mother's company for a while, so I am more than happy to obey her orders. I take the root beer and proceed out of the kitchen, apparently to fix something I didn't even understand was broken.

"So," I say as I approach Liana, "I got your root beer."

"Thanks," she says. She takes the bottle without looking at me.

"It's cold. It's in glass. Not plastic."

"These are all observations I made myself," she says.

"So apparently I've screwed up," I say. Liana doesn't answer. "I mean, you told me about your sister. I was supposed to tell you about my father, I guess."

Finally Liana looks up. "I really don't get that. After

154

everything I've told you, I just don't get how you could hold that back."

"Well, this is what I meant. I didn't get that I owed you a—"

"Christ, Hank, you didn't owe me anything! But it's something we have in common! You know? It's something that would have made me feel closer to you instead of like a million miles away!"

"I'm right here," I say. "Where else would I be?"

Liana looks at me, opens her mouth, closes it, then smiles. "Well," she says, "it is your house, after all."

"Exactly. Mother has worked hard preparing dinner, and Chase took the unusual step of staying sober until dinnertime and I . . . I just want you to eat with us. All I did was buy the root beer."

"I appreciate it. Let's go eat."

"Great. I asked Mother to prepare us some guacamole, but she refused to purchase a stone mortar for the occasion."

"Well, I find guacamole makes an unsatisfying meal anyway."

I want to explain that I didn't mean we should have guacamole for the entire meal. I want to explain to her the beauty of the guacamole preparation ritual, the itch in my brain it scratches, but then I look at her. She's smiling at me. I take this to mean she's not angry. And so I decide to quit while I'm ahead and just smile back at her.

CHAPTER 15
LIANA

"You never did this before?" Hank grunts. He shows up at my door this afternoon, presumably after checking Espresso Love and finding that our usual table was minus one. I wanted to be pissed—and really I was—I mean, who neglects to mention that their dad died? During the dinner at his house I learned that a) his mother is much cooler than my parents could ever be, complete with tattoo and former punk past, and b) Chase is still a lothario, and c) Hank's dad died, and d) his dad died, and e) all of the above, and his dad died and he never told me, even when I told him about Jenny. So I sat with my telescope, staring up at the Seven Sisters cluster, the constellation that most people totally overlook in favor of the Big Dipper, and let the anger roil through my limbs. But then it occurred to me: I never told him what I was supposed to, either. At Planet Guitar I just hesitated and then got blown away by his playing, so I semi-forgot. And then at the dinner I was so shocked by the dead-dad thing that I couldn't even begin to process the words "I cannot kiss you." So I never said anything.

"Here, move like this," Hank says, biting his lower lip in concentration. He turns me by the waist so I'm level with the wall and better able to reach. "So did you? Do this before, I mean?"

"Never," I say, and try not to hurt him as I stand on his palms and grasp the basement window.

"I would have," he says, supporting me, and holding steady as I wedge the speaker into the window frame. "I've almost got it." Hank showed up at the side door of the house and right away asked if we could go to the basement, which didn't mean what it meant when Jett Alterman came over and wanted to "go to the basement." Most of the time when guys ask things, it's in quotes, like "go for a walk," "see my paintings," "hear me play 'Going to California,'" or "see what your room looks like." But Hank just meant go to the basement.

"Careful! Ouch." He winces, and I look over my shoulder to signal at him to let me down.

But he doesn't get my signal, so I say, "Let me down now, Hank," and he does.

"We did it." We stand in the dank darkness of the basement, admiring our handiwork. On Hank's suggestion, we lugged the huge ancient speakers from the storage area over to the windows so we could listen to my parents' old records outside on the porch. The turntable is down here and I wasn't about to try and undo the system, but Hank knew just how to fix the problem.

"There are quite a number of records here," Hank says, and slumps onto the floor across from the small room where the boiler, heating, and AC system sound alive, churning and whirring all night long. "You've got ELP—'Lucky Man' is not bad, you've got every Dylan. Wow—shit—imported *London Calling*—that's worth money, not that I'd sell it, but you could. Like online or something." He plows through one of the cardboard boxes labeled on the side in my mother's writing, the ultra-ambiguous "stuff."

I join Hank and place my hands on the side of the box. "I think they used to keep all this upstairs, lining the floors, or something. But it all got moved to the basement . . ."

"But they didn't throw it away. That's good. You shouldn't trash things just because they aren't current." I look to see if he means more than just records, like old friends, or dead family members, or people you rolled around with on your bed and then never spoke to again, but he doesn't. He just means records, I guess.

Hank's face is intense as he studies the liner notes from a Talking Heads album. Underneath the records are other items: obsolete cords and wires, slips of paper, photographs. Hank picks up a pile of the papers and puts them on the floor between us.

I begin sorting through things, first halfheartedly, crumpling up things we just have no reason to keep. "Look— seems they were out of dish soap. And apples. And cinnamon. Maybe she was making apple crisp or something." I point to the grocery list. On yellow lined paper my mother's old script is underlined. Clearly the spices were crucial.

"Did she always bake?" Hank asks, still clutching a couple records.

I shrug. "I don't know. I think so." Then I sniff, sure I can smell the apple crisp, the lemon shortbread baking upstairs, even though rationally I know I'm wrong. "I think it kind of helps her."

"Like therapy?"

"Yeah. All that sifting and measuring . . ." My voice trails off.

Hank nods. "Did you know that before Gene Simmons and Ace Frehley and the other guys, Peter and Paul, became KISS, they were in this band called Wicked Lester?"

I laugh and push aside one of my kid drawings, wondering if Hank has a reason for saying this, or if it's just more slightly useless knowledge.

"Do you like KISS?" I ask, and my mouth tangles on the last word. Kiss. Kiss. Kiss. Kiss. Hank opens his mouth to answer, but I cut him off. "Here. Look. That's her." Then I think of my father and his grammar. "That is she. Jenny." Hank takes the photo, holding it carefully by the sides, which strikes me as so sweet since it was shoved away under a pile of moldy albums, tossed aside, but right now, held lovingly by him.

He points to her. "She had lighter hair than you, huh?" I nod. In the picture, Jenny is wheelchair-bound, in a plaid skirt, her head tilted to one side. She is maybe five, but it's hard to know.

For some reason, looking at it, at her, in the grimy basement light where I once kissed Jonah Jacobs, where old records and cast-off items reside, I start to cry. Hank keeps his eyes locked to the photo but carefully moves one of his hands so it rests gently on my forearm. His touch feels like the anchor to this moment, like I could fly off and float away if he weren't here.

I point to her hair. "It was kind of red, I think."

"There's a song by the Eurythmics. 'Jennifer.' It's pretty much just rhythm and Annie Lennox saying 'Jennifer, with your orange hair. Jennifer with your green eyes,' but it's very alluring."

For once, this trivia doesn't feel meaningless. It feels intentional, like he wants to calm me down and also keep talking about her, about this nothing-but-something in my life. "Thanks, Hank." I put my hand, just for a moment, on his and then take it away. We are surrounded by a mess of records, covers, old splatter art of mine, and the photos. "Want to listen to the albums now?"

Hank smiles. "Of course. I'll cue up down here and meet you out there?" He points to the deck. "Bring these." He hands me a few liner notes that include lyrics and background information I've never really contemplated. "And this." He hands me the photo of Jenny.

Outside, while I wait for him on the deck, I remember I'm supposed to be angry at him. That he didn't tell me about his dad. That I'm supposed to be finding a way to tell him what I didn't at the dinner.

"Okay," Hanks says, nearly knocking the screen door off

160

its slide. "This is The Band." He waits for me. "As in 'The Weight,' 'Stagefright'?" I shake my head. He plops down onto the wooden deck and looks up at me as sound crackles through the speakers. I sit down near him, facing the water view, the overly green grass of late summer, and block my eyes from the sun's brightness. Hank's whole body seems to be infected with the music. "You've got the fiddle, tambourine, pump organ, acoustic and electric guitars, piano, bass, and drums . . . and it's just so raw and real, you know?"

I listen to the lyrics and think. I say, "It's like they're afraid of being out there, in front of a crowd, but also out there . . ." I motion to my heart, but Hank looks confused.

"I don't get what you're saying. . . . Do you like it?"

I nod. "Yeah, I do, but what I mean is, even with all those instruments, with the lyrics, they're scared. 'Stagefright.' Not just being booed off or whatever, but with being honest . . . in a song." Hank absorbs every word I'm saying. "You don't pay as much attention to the lyrics, do you?"

Hank tucks his knees to his chest, shielding his eyes with his hand. "I do. No, wait, not like that. I know them. I can quote songs. But I've never . . . I guess when I got into music I was more concerned with the playing, the sound, the history." He stands up. "Time for the next song."

"Aren't we listening to albums?" I imagine Hank frenetic, leaping up after each song to DJ the next one, and realize it's not a very conducive way to have a conversation. "Maybe pick a whole album?"

"But there's so many I want you to hear. Or, if you've heard them, re-hear." He pauses. "With me."

I swallow hard. "I still wish you'd told me about your dad."

Hanks eyes drift away from mine, flitting around anywhere, everywhere, but not on mine. "I didn't think it mattered."

"To you? Or to me? Because I think it matters to both of us." Hank crouches down and The Band continues playing, the banjo twanging out, happy and sad the way banjos always sound. "When I told you about Jenny, back in Chase's room that time . . . that was the time you could've said, Well, actually, Liana, my dad . . ."

Hank presses his fingers into the spaces between the wooden deck planks. "You mean, there's one time to say stuff? It's just too complicated." His voice wavers. "I can't . . . I never know when that time is."

I meet his gaze. "Hank, there isn't just one time. You can say what you want to say—and if you miss an opportunity, you find another one. Like when you played guitar at the store—I didn't know you'd messed up, and even if I had, I wouldn't have cared. But you knew and you kept going. That's the same thing with talking. With telling."

Hank looks like he's going to either fall backward or fall right into me, so I stand up and pull him along with me. "So . . . you want to know about my dad?" he says.

"If you want to tell me," I say. Inside, the timer goes off on my mom's oven items. I head in, my eyes immediately adjusting to the shade as I grab a mitt and take the Pyrex dish from the oven. Hank comes in, the music still going outside.

"I wasn't always into music."

I put the dish on the stove top to cool, the sweet rich buttery smell wafting up into the air. "I can't imagine that. What'd you talk about?" I lean on the kitchen island and watch Hank shift around, tugging on his sleeves, chording on his thighs. I take the photo of Jenny from my back pocket and put it on the counter, lying facedown. Then I flip it over.

"Maps."

I wait for more, but Hank disappears downstairs, and when it's been five minutes and he's still not back, I shout down to the basement. "You okay?"

He mumbles something, and I head out to the deck, this time reclining, lying flat with my face to the sun, my legs exposed and arms tingling with the breezy warmth until a shadow appears over me. I tilt my head back and look up. "Maps? You liked maps?"

Hank sits up next to me, and I can see him eyeing the length of me, my toes up to my hair. "Cartography. Scale models of special concepts. Geographical information conveyed on paper." He twists his mouth, and when I poke his leg, he laughs. "What? I never said I was cool."

"And then what happened?"

Hank scoots to my right and then lies next to me. "Then he died and I rolled up all my maps and all paraphernalia that went with them and . . ." He pauses. "I never knew him. Not well. Not like you're supposed to."

I blow my bangs off my forehead, and Hank sits saying nothing—nothing—for a whole minute, then chords briefly. I thumb my tattoo in response, tracing the planets and then covering the skin with my tank top. The needle scratches inside, and Hank jumps up, bounds away, fixes the record player, and slides right back where he was, but maybe just a fraction closer, so our legs are touching. From above, we must look like gingerbread people, all cutouts of arms and legs.

"This is that song," he says. "The one I told you about at dinner? The Kinks." The music starts. "'Waterloo Sunset.'"

We lie there, the chords distilling into the air, away from us but hovering in the heat. The lyrics make my heart pound: boy meets girl at the train station and finally kiss as the sun sets. The sun is a few hours from setting here, in non-song world, but our bodies are close. "It's really good, isn't it?" Hank asks, rolling his head so we're looking right at each other.

"It is," I say. "What comes next?"

Hank smiles. "The same song. I put it on repeat."

I sigh and laugh at the same time. "Why? I always like to hear other ones . . ."

"Certain songs are so good that you want to hear them again, right away. Get to know them . . . like in the middle, how the tone dips but then they speed up the sound and—"

I listen to the song as it starts up again. Instead of feeling annoyed that I'm re-hearing everything, I listen more. "So we're just going to listen to this?" I ask. Hank nods. His eyes are intensely beautiful, his mouth so ripe, his fingers chording on his thighs but reverberating on mine.

"Sometimes," Hanks says slowly, "I like to hear a song and then deconstruct it. So I know everything about it. Then

I put it together again and it's . . ." He looks at me. "Mine. Or something."

We stay there, still as a photograph, as two lovers in London meet at the train station in song around us. And then, right as I hear my mother's keys in the side door, but before she finds the picture of Jenny, I move my hand onto Hank's. He breathes in deeply, as though he's trying also to inhale me, or us, or the whole day.

"Hank," I say, and squeeze his hand before I sit up. "We can't kiss, okay?"

CHAPTER 16
HANK

Double you tee eff. This is a text-message abbreviation you're supposed to use when you're confused. Such as when you are lying down with your girlfriend, holding hands, the mother of all boners threatening to split your pants in half, and she leans over with her soft skin and her hair falling down and touching your skin and you want her to open her mouth so you can just crawl right inside and be the same person and then she tells you you can't kiss.

That is when you say double you tee eff.

I do not say double you tee eff. Instead I start trying to figure things out.

I look at Liana. I don't think she's cynical like Chase, but it seems clear that she feels somewhat betrayed by my lack of forthrightness on the dead-father issue, even after I explained about that. She says I don't owe her anything, but it would draw us closer. The distinction she's making is unclear to me, but being closer to her sounds pretty good. So I decide to be completely forthright.

"My parents met at a Rollins Band concert. My father was—well, he grew up before the diagnosis, but it seems clear to both Mother and myself that he was . . . like me. Nana and Grandpa did not know what to make of him. He was obsessed with music, and when he started hanging out at punk rock concerts, they were just happy that he wasn't in the basement with his extensive model train collection, making them uncomfortable anymore. All of this, by the way, comes from Mother, who does not get along with Nana. So perhaps we can take it all with a grain of salt.

"In any case, when my father died, I felt it was appropriate that I should . . . carry on the music obsession. But also. Here is the part I don't like talking about."

"Hank," Liana says. "You don't have to—"

But I kind of do, and in any case, now that I've started, I think it would be difficult for me to stop.

"We would sit side by side for hours, you know, him cataloging his music collection, me sharing interesting tidbits about, for example, the ever-shifting borders of certain African nations. This was . . ."

My voice is breaking, and Liana is propped up on an elbow looking at me, but I can't look at her.

"I know that this was his way of expressing love. I think he was as puzzled by Chase as Mother is by me. He would attend the games and cheer, but fundamentally not get it. So I know . . . I know he loved me. I know he loved me because he would sit with me and listen to me talk about maps, and because he would tell me the history of SST Records the way some parents tell the story of Goldilocks and the Three Bears.

"But all the same, he never took me in his arms and hugged me and told me he loved me so much, the way Mother does.

"And this is why I listen to music. Because I miss him terribly. All the time. Time is supposed to heal these things, that's what I've read, but it hasn't seemed to work that way for me."

And there are tears in my eyes, which is embarrassing. But then Liana's hand is wiping a tear from my cheek. This is a gesture I understand completely. It makes me smile.

She reaches down and gives my hand a squeeze, and we lie side by side not speaking. I hear Ray Davies say again that he doesn't feel afraid.

But I do, Ray. I feel afraid because when you love someone, when you feel that they understand you and want to spend time with you, then they go away. This is what happens.

I'm having a hard time stopping the tears. I suppose I let them out so very infrequently that there is quite a buildup. Also, I've never quite faced up to what feels like the inevitability of Liana's departure from my life. One way or another, it's going to happen. I squeeze her hand. Maybe if I can only hold it tight enough I'll never have to let go.

I hear the back door open, but I don't open my eyes. I don't want to display red eyes to Liana's mother and face a lot of questions. So I lie with my eyes closed. I'm almost certain this is rude.

"I've got some lemon shortbread if you guys are interested!" Liana's mother says.

Liana gives my hand a squeeze, gets up, and walks over to her mother. They have a quiet conversation, which ends with Liana's mother leaving quickly and stomping her feet louder than she did when she came in.

I hear Liana sit down next to me. She takes my hand again. "Hey," she says. "You okay?"

"'I am in paradise,'" I sing along with Ray Davies. Liana laughs.

"Yeah, that's usually how I feel when I have tears running down my cheeks," she says, then says quietly, "but I know what you mean."

We don't say anything for a while. I've already said more than I've said in years. It occurs to me that I may have just completely exhausted my supply of words. Maybe I'll never say anything again. I wonder idly if this would make my life easier or harder.

"I just . . . I want you to know," Liana says, "that it's not because of you. It's because of me. The reason I can't kiss you. I just . . . they were . . ." She takes a breath and shakes her hair. "I've kissed a lot of guys, Hank. A *lot*. But none of them were . . . I never . . . This"—she points to me and then back to her herself—"is better than all that. And I just don't understand myself, you know? I don't know why I kiss boys and run away from them, and I'm afraid if I kiss you I'll run away from you too. And I don't want to do that."

"That would suck," I say. It appears I have some words left in me after all.

"I'm sorry, Hank. You're really . . . You deserve . . . I guess, I mean, I don't know what you think. I know it probably sounds nuts, but I have to prove to myself that the note isn't true; I have to figure out what the hell's wrong with me. I guess I . . . well, you're a guy, so you'll probably want to bail, and I guess I can't blame you."

It takes me a moment to realize what she means. She assumes that I'm like Chase; that I will feel she's not upholding her end of the exchange, and I will therefore want to stop spending time with her. It occurs to me that she has no idea what I'm thinking or feeling, and I wonder how she could be so clueless. Perhaps this is how people feel when they talk to me. She thinks that if I spend time with her with no hope of kissing her (well, no immediate hope. Surely this period of self-discovery that precludes kissing can't last forever), I would naturally prefer to return to hanging out alone with no hope of kissing anyone ever.

"It's going to be a lot harder than that to get rid of me." Finally I chance to look at Liana. She's looking at me. "I'm like John Oates. I'll always be there, even if nobody really understands what I do."

"I don't know who that is," she says. Her eyes are right on mine.

"Few people do. He is half of Hall and Oates. They are a kind of white pop soul duo. They were big in the '80s. Except that Daryl Hall writes and sings all the songs. And G. E. Smith handled most of the lead guitar duties. So what, exactly, is Oates doing there? Nobody knows, but Daryl Hall has put out solo albums without him, and nobody buys them."

"So he's mysterious, yet indispensable."

"It would appear so."

I look at her, and for just a moment I understand something social. Liana is caught in a contradiction. She wants to kiss me for agreeing not to kiss her. Which of course would thwart her plans to abstain from kissing.

There are a number of blogs written by people with Asperger's and other autism spectrum disorders. They refer to the autism *community*, which strikes me as a humorously oxymoronic phrase, and they write often about our "wonderful difference." My reaction upon reading this in the past has always been that anyone who thinks this, or for that matter any, difference is wonderful has obviously never attended an American middle school.

And yet here, watching Liana sort through the puzzle of multiple meanings and intentions that seems to constitute her social life, I feel grateful for my utter ignorance of such things. I may not understand much about the way other people work, but I don't have to second-guess myself. I want to be with Liana even if our relationship is different. Because it's wonderful.

Eventually I wind up back at my own house, having exchanged hand squeezes rather than kisses with Liana. It occurs to me that if hand squeezing were the defining gesture of intimacy rather than kissing, I would not feel that there was anything missing from our relationship. Except if that were true, Liana would have tearfully admitted to having squeezed a lot of hands and would have kissed me good night, leaving me longing for a hand squeeze.

I am not particularly jealous of the fact that Liana has kissed a *lot* of guys. After all, she likes me better. And, really, if she had kissed me and fled, I would have been ecstatic for a couple of days, and then summer would have returned to its normal routine of loneliness and obsessing about music.

I lie in my bed and cannot sleep. Masturbation is normally a pretty good sleep aid, but tonight it only serves to make me more hyper. (Since discovering that I possess the skill necessary to disguise my fantasies from the outside world, I've been rather unstoppable in this area.)

Finally, I get up and wander down to the basement. I plug headphones into the amp, plug in my Gibson, and begin to play. I try "Pipeline," but it doesn't sound right on this guitar, and anyway it doesn't really capture the way I'm feeling. I try "Waterloo Sunset," which gets closer but is still not on the mark.

I search my mental catalogs. Surely someone has written a song that perfectly captures all of the contradictory emotions I'm feeling—the longing for Liana's touch that feels like a physical pain, the happiness about having her in my life tinged with sadness at the knowledge that nothing is permanent. I can't remember ever feeling so many emotions so strongly in my life. Certainly I have felt grief and loss so strong I thought they would destroy me, but I've never felt this bittersweet wonderful sad happiness before.

I pluck the harmonics like I'm going to play Yes's "Round-about," but this is just absent-minded strumming. There is not an intoxicant powerful enough to make me feel that a song about becoming a traffic circle relates to me.

There is no song that relates to how I feel. I'm losing myself: she's the sun, and I'm just a planet orbiting her. Or, more accurately, I'm a moon orbiting a Planet.

I tiptoe upstairs and grab a notebook and pen from my book bag, and tiptoe back into the basement, where I play guitar until I can hear the song. The song about Liana and me. With some effort I pull it from the air through the guitar and manage to transcribe it.

It was always complete, but after an hour, Liana's song is also complete on the page and on the tape deck I've hooked up to the amp. I have to be at work in four hours. I am exhausted. I've never felt better in my life.

I wake up three and a half hours later, and the first thing I do is look over the lyrics to the song I wrote last night. They are mawkish, clumsy, and embarrassing. It's possible that what seems like genius at four a.m. may turn out to be excrement in the cold light of day, which is, of course, when I'll be playing at Beachfest. I rip up the lyrics and throw the scraps away. I'll try again tonight.

CHAPTER 17
LIANA

Nothing says fun like getting pelted in the face with a wet sponge.

"Hey, asshole, chuck it over here," Chase says to some guy who is pretending to fix his flip-flop but is really crouching down for protection from the water-dodgeball masses. I look around for Hank but he still hasn't shown up. Chase said, "Hank? He's working. Or sleeping. Or something, but he told me he'd show up," and then convinced me to follow the summer lemmings and take part in this demented version of gym class.

I fling an oversized wet blue sponge at some girl who just whipped it at my back, and allow myself to get caught up in the mayhem of summer. I defend myself, running, twisting, trying to avoid being the body target for the continual barrage of soaking sponges. There's a mix of people at Chase's friend's house—the kind of odd blender of schools and ages that you can only find in the summer. Chase's crew from college, a herd from my high school, unfamiliar people from Hank's, some kids whose parents have summer homes here. On the lawn, with all of us dripping, our T-shirts clinging and our hair plastered to our heads in the blaring sunshine, we're all just one cluster, though.

"Hey, Liana, catch this!" I look up just in time to catch a sponge—heavy with water—with my face. Reeling slightly, I regain my sight after I wipe the liquid off, only to find Hank as the culprit.

"Ow, Hank, that hurt," I say to him. He's in long sleeves and jeans despite the fact that its eighty degrees and there are more tank tops and bathing suits on display than in a catalogue.

Hank shrugs, shifting his weight from one foot to the other. "Everyone's throwing them." He picks up the offending sponge from the grass.

Instinctively, I flinch lest he throw it again. "Yeah, but you chucked it at close range." We stand there for a few seconds not saying anything while the shrieks of glee echo around us.

"Quite an arm there, buddy." Pren Stevens, shirtless and grinning, jogs by on his way to douse someone with a bucket of water. "You should go out for varsity!"

"Varsity what?" Hank asks him, not realizing it was a rhetorical comment. I swallow, feeling the blood begin to pump faster through my heart, all four chambers working overtime so I don't freak out when I notice that not only

175

is Pren here, but Jett Alterman too. And over by the keg, which someone has elaborately draped with a beach towel as though that will disguise its function and illicit nature, Mitch Palmer is filling his cup. With a couple of deep breaths I will myself not to panic. They are just boys. Boys whose lips have been on mine, some in the dark, others under the bleachers in broad daylight, or outside the candy shop where I stood with Hank. Hank. I look at him.

He's staring at something off a ways. "Do you have a bathing suit?" I ask him. My nose hurts from the sponge-whack, but I try to ignore it.

"No." Hank crosses his arms. "I'm not a swimmer."

"I didn't mean to swim," I say, and wave back when Summer Sanderson, every inch her name, waves to me before her bikinified body is drenched with ice water. I only know Summer from a chem lab last year, but at parties like this, it feels as though everyone could be your long-lost buddy, that each person is part of this larger mass of cells, or so-lar systems, connected, if only by the space between them. I sigh and then punch Hank on the arm. "Come on, Hank, just loosen up and get wet." I grab a sponge from near my bare feet and toss it around, trying to tempt him with play.

"Chase is loaded," Hank says, pointing to his brother, who has a Frisbee balanced on his head, but still plays dodgeball.

I shrug. "Maybe he's just inebriated with fun." I squint and then laugh as Chase takes a running leap on the wet slicked grass and slides toward a group of girls.

"I'm a human bowling ball!" Chase shouts as he knocks the girls over.

A bright pink sponge thwacks me in the stomach. I catch it and immediately throw it in the direction whence it came. "Don't even think about nailing me in the chest," I say as James Frenti, all surfer shorts and glowing from his day job at the community pool, eases by us.

"You never know when you're gonna get splashed here!" he says, eyeing Hank.

I wonder how he sees him. Us. A couple? A girl he kissed and some guy dressed wrong who won't play the game? Despite everyone being connected here, I see the guys I've fooled around with as sort of bright spots on a map. The places I could mark with a thumbtack. This hits me as hard as the sponge: that kissing someone, marking them like I just envisioned, is just another way of saying you've been somewhere. That you are somewhere. That you exist.

"Who's that?" Hank asks as James sponges his next victim, Nicola Breuner. In a bright yellow tank top with crisscrossing straps, Nicola giggles. No doubt she'll secure the coveted Most Personable spot in the yearbook, always smiling and cheerful, even to me, and she hardly knows me.

I pull my T-shirt away from my body, trying to unslick it from my skin. Hank watches with great interest, and I grin at him. "That's just a guy. James." Hank doesn't say anything else, so I keep going, being honest with him as always, as though we're back on the porch and no one else is around. I lower my voice. "One of the guys I told you about. The kissing?" I sigh. "He totally suffers from lead-singer syndrome. Plays in that band Alligator Smile." James lets Nicola go and careens toward a cheerleader from my school. "Not worth the price of admission."

Hank surveys the crowd, his fingers chording faster. "Isn't that the guy—the one we saw on the beach that night?"

"Stop pointing!" I knock Hank's hand down from its prominent and obvious position. "Yeah, Jett Alterman."

"Let me guess—another, um, lead singer?"

Water drips from my ponytail onto my back; from my bangs down my cheeks. The sun is hard on my face. "Yeah. As I said, there are people here . . ." Chase waves to us from a ways down the hill. I give a halfhearted wave back.

"Yeah, it's really crowded." Hank checks over his shoulder like he's scouting for muggers.

My voice fills with annoyance. Not so much at him, but at him with me. We stick out now, where I was just a few minutes ago blending in with the atmosphere. "It's just a party, okay?"

Hank keeps chording, immune to the tumble of people behind him, all piling atop one another, a wet version of Twister on the grass. "The music sucks."

I try to hear it, but it's just a bass rumble overtaken by chatter, and screeches, and some girl yelling, "Oh my God! Oh my God!" as she's willingly carried on some guy's back. "I don't think people are here for the music," I say.

"Hey!" Chase runs over. "Come to the kitchen—rumor has it someone's grilling steak!" He smiles, wiping his face on the shirt in his hands. "Glad you came, bro." He studies

Hank then turns to me. "He's trying to get out more, you know? Like, try new things?"

I nod, feeling a mixture of frustration that Chase is talking to me as though Hank's not here, and disappointment when I realize he's kind of right: Hank's blank stare makes it feel as if there were miles between us. "Hank—let's get something to eat, okay? I've been in the sun too long anyway."

We head inside, where the shock of cold air is nothing compared to walking smack into Mitch Palmer and Margo Rattner making out by the fridge. When you've kissed someone, had them shirtless against your own shirtlessness, and then you see them pressed into someone else—it's beyond weird. It's not just like being replaced, but like you were never there. So I mentally take out the thumbtack I created before.

My Littered Kisses tour is virtually assembled at this party, and my brain is on overdrive. "I gotta go to the bathroom. I'll be right back," I tell Hank and Chase. I head to the small powder room at the back of the house, take a few breaths, and ignore my disheveled state. When I emerge, I am a bit more relaxed. Until I find Hank deep in conversational throes with Pren Stevens.

"But Helium has street cred," Pren says as he crunches on baby carrots and dip.

"Who's talking about street cred?" Hank answers. "Jude Mission can't drum for shit, and Martin Lewis didn't even write the lyrics."

"But they rock." Pren shrugs. "And if download sales

are anything to go by, other people see my point."

I let them duke it out, feeling my cheeks blaze. Pren doesn't know about me and Hank. Does anyone? Does it matter? I fiddle with some ice, scooping it into a cup and reaching for the soda.

Hank sees me next to him and stops me in mid-pour. "You don't like Coke," he says. Pren raises his eyebrows, suddenly cluing in. The soda dribbles onto the granite countertop and drips onto my feet.

Chase hands me a towel. "Anyone want a burger?"

"Sure," I say as I mop up the sticky soda and put the cup back on the counter. By the sink, someone's saying something about Beachfest, and Pren is disagreeing in that way only guys do, all "No no no, dude, you gotta play hard and then follow with a . . ."

"Are you ready for Beachfest?" I ask Hank.

"Dude, you're playing?" Some guy I don't recognize raises a glass to Hank.

"Who is that?" I ask.

Chase answers for Hank. "Judd Parrish—lacrosse player."

Hank shrugs, saying to no one and everyone, "Yeah—I mean, I think I am. No, I am. Playing at Beachfest." He turns to me. "I gotta find the stereo system and switch this crap." I watch him saunter off.

Nicola smiles at me and reaches for the Coke bottle. "Hey, Liana." She takes a sip. "Nice to see you out and about."

I nod. "I'm glad to be out of the lab."

Her skin is a deep bronze, her hair somehow not matted,

still perky. "That's right. I heard you were doing some research thing?"

"Extra credit," I explain as a few of Nicola's friends come into the room. They stand in a girl huddle, all pressed together, conferring over something. "Colleges, all that."

Nicola nudges her friend Claire, who nudges back. They laugh. "Fine," Nicola says, acquiescing, "I'll ask." She swivels to face me again. "So . . . what's the deal with the snowman over there?" She points to Hank.

"The snowman?"

Nicola's friends laugh. "I mean, it's like a zillion degrees. Isn't he . . . hot?"

I could say he's got a skin condition or something else to shut them up, but I don't. Instead I just shrug. "He's out of tank tops." Nicola laughs good-naturedly. Hank returns to where we are and proceeds to sift through the snack bags, no doubt looking for pretzel sticks, which are about the only salty item he likes. Chase wolfs his second burger, taking a turn at the grill.

Nicola grabs a handful of chips and notices Hank's rummaging, but decides to ignore it.

Pren leans on the counter, talking to all of us, but looking at me like he's picturing the way my mouth tasted, making me wobble. Nicola flinches like someone stepped on her little toe, and I'm hit with the knowledge that she was the one I'd seen him with outside Espresso Love. That maybe they're a couple. That maybe I'm intruding. Or did before. I lean back, looking for Hank, but he's rearranging the burger Chase gave him, removing the bun and adding mustard.

Nicola steps in. "So, Liana. What else have you been up to this summer?" she asks, her voice ever placid but her lips stretched taut on her teeth. "You know, aside from extra credit." She says extra credit as though it means blow job.

"Basically, I'm all about the extra credit," I say, wondering what I'm implying. "Planetary science, lunar cycles, stars."

"You always were a brain," Pren butts in, hoisting himself onto the counter so he's between me and Nicola.

Why can't it be normal to talk to him? Just because you've kissed someone doesn't mean the air between you is permanently altered or anything. I let my eyes rest on his lips, remembering how it felt when he wrapped his arms around my back, how he whispered onto my neck. I focus again on his eyes, remembering, too, how when the kiss ended with him, I felt kind of empty, like you do after eating only candy. You know you've had food, but it hasn't registered.

Nicola tugs on Claire's tank top. "But not only work, right? Looks like you've had some play." She raises her eyebrows toward Hank. So much for Most Personable.

Hank's back by the stereo, locked in verbal combat with whoever is controlling it. I wave to him, trying to stay calm, but also needing him near. Everything with Hank is so not what I had or didn't have with Pren. Or Jett. Or anyone. But no one can see that here.

"That kid knows nothing about music," Hank complains, coming over. "He won't let me play 'Hot Fun in the Summertime.'" I give my best wide-eyed drop-it signal to Hank, but he goes on. "I gotta hear 'Hot Fun in the Summertime.'"

I lower my voice, reaching for his hand, but he's too

fidgety to find mine. "Hank, no one cares about Sly and the Family Stone right now."

"See?" He pats my back. "You know the band, at least."

"I want you to meet someone," I tell him. There are my past kisses. Past hookups. But they have nothing on me now. When I see the lips, the boys, it's like flipping through a photo album—memories mingled with moments, but not what I need now. The strength builds inside me as I bring Hank into the group.

"Hank, this is Pren. Stevens," I add as though his last name matters.

"Right, we were talking before." Hank nods but goes back to his fixation. "This was really the end of the hippie version of Sly and the Family Stone. After this comes the 'Thank You Falletin Me Be Mice Elf Again' single, and then, of course, 'There's a Riot Going On,' which was titled that as an answer to Marvin Gaye's 'What's Going On.'"

What's going on is Hank being ostentatiously weird. I wish he would stop the music trivia. Nicola looks at him with a mixture of curiosity and disdain. "Nice to meet you, Hank. I'm Nicola." She takes his hand and lets it linger in hers, giving me a look that explains it all. I am the bad girl. The one who got to Pren before she did. The one who should leave. But it wasn't like that. I want to explain to her that it wasn't a big deal. That Pren didn't—doesn't—mean enough to fight over.

Pren pops down from the counter, shaking Hank's hand and adding, "Hey, I guess you know your stuff. But here's the fifty thousand dollar question." Hank waits. "Ice Cube sampled 'Sing a Simple Song' four different times—betcha didn't know that."

For all of one minute, everything's fine. We are two girls with their musically inclined guys all swarming in a summer kitchen. Pren sings in his overly dramatic way—the way that only seemed overly dramatic after we'd kissed and I realized how little there was to support his exterior. "I'm going for another round o' sponging. You game?" He asks Nicola or me or both, but she demurely declines, and I pretend not to have heard the invite.

Hank squeezes my hand. I feel good about introducing him. As if this solidifies where I am now. With Hank. With my pact. Chase eats his burger and watches us—protectively, maybe. Everything is fine. "I'll be right back," I say to Hank, and go to try and convince the DJ to give it up already and play Hank's song. I watch Hank while I'm across the room—smiling as he successfully converses with Nicola and her group of girls, managing to enthrall them with music trivia or whatever else springs to mind.

When I walk back over, I say, "Well, he's going to play your song."

And before Hank can respond, Nicola busts out laughing. "And we know all about yours."

Claire laughs too. I'm confused, and I look at Hank for an explanation. Claire tilts her head, leaning in toward me, "What is your song, exactly?"

"She doesn't have a song," Nicola says, and giggles. "At least not this summer, right?"

Blush overtakes my face. "What do you mean?"

Hank waves Nicola's comments off as though the words are swattable—mere mosquitoes. "She's just meaning the kissing thing." I stare at Hank, dread rising up my legs, fear and embarrassment filling my insides.

"Hank?" My voice comes out warbled as "Hot Fun in the Summertime" starts up in the background.

Nicola blurts out, "It's quite a pact you have going with yourself."

"Yeah," Claire agrees. "Talk about rules and regulations. Did you have to run the no-kissing thing by a board of directors?"

Nicola guffaws. "No. It's popular vote."

The room seems to come to a complete standstill. Hank's eyes wander as soon as he hears the music, his body registering it. I poke him on the arm. "Hank?"

Hank finally responds. "I figured it's okay. You know, they're your friends. The girls?" I stand there, so exposed I feel I could melt. Pren Stevens stands at the sliding-glass door. I grip Hank's forearm, willing him to shut up, but he adds his final remark, sealing me in a pit of embarrassment. "Look, Liana, it's no big thing. I told them that the note that said you're a slut doesn't mean anything, okay?"

Hank's words bring the room to a full stop. Pren flinches and turns away, shaking his head. Nicola stares so hard at me it feels like I've been hit with the sponge again, but this time it's not water dripping down my face, it's shame.

"Nice." Chase elbows his brother and looks at me to make sure I'm okay.

Which I am, but I'm not sure what to do. So I'm only

kind of okay. Which means I'm not. I glare at Hank. I wish for something to say. Something funny, self-deprecating, to gloss over it, so the girls with yearbook-worthy nicknames let all of this go.

"Dude," Chase says to Hank.

Hank looks at the wreckage in front of us—the scowls from me, the crossed-arm defiance from Nicola, Claire's wicked grin, a bit of disgust from a few onlookers—and shakes his head. "I don't get it."

Finally I know what to say. I glance at Chase and the rest of the room, and tell Hank, "Neither do I," before I bolt.

CHAPTER 18
HANK

Liana storms away from the party. I guess I won't be getting a good-night kiss, ha-ha.

Chase is at my elbow, the booze reeking from his breath. "Dude," he says, "you are such a tool. How could you do that to her?"

"Chase, you'll forgive me if I don't take your advice on how to treat girls seriously. Run along and do something you're good at. There are probably two or three girls with tramp stamps at this party who you haven't slept with yet. Oh, wait, I think you did sleep with that girl in the red bikini. Was she the one you called butterface? What's a butterface anyway?"

I know what a butterface is because I made Chase explain it to me after he'd dumped the girl in the red bikini. "Her body's smokin' hot," he'd said, "but her *face* . . ." I also know that taunting Chase when he is drunk may lead to fisticuffs. I feel that I need to get back on familiar ground, socially speaking, after having just navigated the rock-fouled waters of a high school party and not only running aground, but possibly sinking the ship. I make fun of Chase in ways he's not smart enough to counter. He hits me. Cause and effect. It's like Mother with the yelling, the apology, and the sweet boy. It's a comfortable, familiar pattern. And maybe I deserve it. Maybe I just want him to punish me for making Liana cry.

Three things happen in quick succession: 1.) As expected, Chase punches me in the face. He hits me hard, just below the eye. 2.) Butterface runs from the party in tears. I wonder if I should have said that. It never occurred to me that I might hurt an innocent bystander in my effort to hurt Chase. 3.) One of the guys Liana kissed—I honestly can't remember their names or tell them apart, as they all seem to be only slightly different versions of the same person, but this one had Butterface on his arm until she ran from the party—hits Chase.

One of the other kiss boys—if they would at least wear makeup like the members of the band KISS, I would be able to tell them apart—yells, "Hell, yeah! Now it's a party!" and jumps into the fray.

Some girl screams. I hear glass breaking. Someone else punches me in the side of the head. Is it Chase? One of the members of KISS? I don't know, but as I hit the ground, I look for platform boots and see none. I begin crawling away from the mêlée. The mêlée I caused. Someone appears to have spilled beer on my head. I put my hand up to my head and wonder when they started making beer red.

I keep crawling until I reach a point where I believe it will be possible for me to stand. I see flip-flop-clad feet, toes with rings on them, and the beginnings of tanned, shiny, smooth female legs.

"Nice job, dork!" one of the girls yells down at me. "Way to wreck the party!"

I pick myself up and find myself a little unsteady. "Thank you," I say. "I am available to ruin any party for a small fee." It occurs to me that this might be a valuable service to offer. Perhaps I will put an ad on Craigslist. It might allow me to earn enough for a Jazzmaster. Anything is possible.

After a few steps I start feeling slightly better. Then I stop and vomit. This has the surprising effect of clearing my head somewhat. I am walking alone down the streets of Melville. After five minutes or so, a Melville police cruiser passes me, doubtless on the way to the party. I wonder idly if Chase will get arrested and whether I care.

I want to go home, but I can't. Mother will surely be there, and in a house the size of ours, it is very unlikely I will be able to get to the basement and the guitars, to the world I understand, without another stop in the world I don't understand: Mother will see my wounds, clean me up, coax the story from me, and lecture me about how one must behave in a relationship.

This is not a conversation I am eager to have.

I walk to Planet Guitar, hoping I can at least use the employee bathroom to wash the blood from my hair. I open the door, jingling the bell attached to it. I hear Stan's voice from the back.

"We're just closing up," he says.

"It's me!" I call out.

"Hank?" Stan says, and he emerges from the back and says, "Jesus Christ! What happened to you?"

"I suppose I was in a fight," I say. This has a more macho sound to it than, "I was punched twice."

"I guess so," he says. "Let me guess. Something to do with the hottie who was in here the other day."

"Something to do with her, yes," I say.

"Welcome to the fun-filled world of relationships. Here," Stan says, reaching behind the counter. He tosses me the first-aid kit, a white plastic lunchbox with a red cross on it. "You might need some stitches on that head, but I think there are some butterfly closures in there. Just, you know, just because you're getting first aid here doesn't mean you can file for workers' comp, though," Stan says.

"I have no intention of filing for workers' comp," I say.

"It was a joke, kid. Go to the bathroom, will you? I don't want you bleeding on the merchandise."

I take the first-aid kit to the bathroom and examine myself. My face is starting to swell, and there is blood in my hair. I wash the blood off and examine the wound. It's a long scratch. My guess is that my second assailant was wearing a watch, and the buckle or some other feature of the timepiece scraped my scalp as the blow glanced off what Chase refers to as my "rock-hard skull." It will not require stitches.

I dry my hair with paper towels, grab the instant cold

pack, squeeze it to activate it, and put it on my face. I rip open a condom-wrapper-sized packet of ibuprofen and pop the contents into my mouth. I emerge from the bathroom and hand the first-aid kit to Stan, who's standing in front of a stack of amps, holding a very nice Les Paul.

"Trade you," he says, handing me the Jazzmaster as he takes the first-aid kit. "You're gonna have a hell of a shiner there. Pretty rock and roll. What do you want to play, killer?"

"KISS," I say.

"The Prince song or the band?" he asks.

"The band," I say, handing him back the Jazzmaster. It's not right for the songs, and anyway, playing it feels too sad now, since the last time I played it was for Liana. Now it's like a relationship with Liana—something I wanted so bad I could scream, and something that is now out of my reach. "I think I'm gonna need a Les Paul for the Ace Frehley parts."

Stan laughs. "Dude, you are totally taking me back to my misspent youth." He pauses for a moment. "You know what? I'm gonna call a couple of the guys I misspent it with. Tune up a Washburn for me, will you?"

I tune the Washburn—it was actually designed by Paul Stanley and looks very metal.

Stan comes back. "All right, Ace. I got Gene and Peter on the way. They're actually Al and Mike. I'm afraid we're gonna have to let Al sing, though."

"Lead-singer syndrome," I say, not really knowing what it means. I feel a twinge—it's Liana's phrase.

"Totally," Stan says.

I call Mother and tell her Stan will drop me off after I'm

done jamming with him and some friends. There is a long silence. "Are you doing drugs?" Mother says.

"Yes," I reply. "I have taken four hundred milligrams of ibuprofen. Stan actually gave it to me. Would you like to verify my story with him?"

"No, smart-ass," Mother says. "Just tell me you're not playing country music."

"It's not country, Mother."

"Okay. Just remember you're not named after Hank Williams, damn it."

"I will, Mother." Sometimes on weekend nights when she's not working, Mother sits up late, with a big goblet of Merlot, and looks at old photo albums and cries. I wonder if I've interrupted this activity and whether that's a good thing or a bad thing.

Stan busies himself setting up a drum kit, and I find myself with a few minutes in which to think. This does not please me.

I wonder if people can change. Chase is the same as he's ever been. Mother has been in mourning for five years. Liana wanted me to reinvent myself, as did Chase. They cajoled me into attending a party where I knew I wouldn't have any fun, and sure enough, apart from hearing "Hot Fun in the Summertime," I didn't have any fun and spoiled everyone else's fun to boot. Now Liana is mad at me for having a disability. Which is what her anger amounts to. It's as though she brought a guy in a wheelchair to a party and got mad that he couldn't dance. Or if she got angry at the fish out of water for being unable to breathe. I don't think I will ever be able to successfully negotiate a party like that. I don't think I will ever want to be able to do that.

Which of course brings up the question of whether Liana will be able to change. It seems important to her to be able to stop kissing boys and to run away from them. Well, so far so good, I suppose; she's run away from me without kissing me. Perhaps there's hope after all.

Al arrives, quickly followed by Mike. They are Stan's age, have gray hair, and are thick around the middle. It occurs to me that they are younger than the actual members of KISS.

"We played all KISS covers at the tenth grade Harvest Fair. Makeup and everything," Stan says.

"Who was Ace?" I say.

"The guy who stole Stan's girlfriend and made her his wife," Mike says from behind the drum kit.

"We're no longer close," Stan says, smiling.

"So kid," Al says. "What songs do you know?"

"I know every song from *Double Platinum*," I say sheepishly. "But if you gentlemen are big *Music from 'The Elder'* fans, I suppose I can fake my way through."

"*Music from 'The—*" Al sputters. I laugh. *Music from "The Elder"* is considered to be the worst of a bad bunch of post-1978 KISS albums, even by the band itself.

"Less talk, more rock," Mike calls. "'Rock and Roll All Nite.'"

I look at the middle-aged men around me. I doubt they would be able to do anything all nite, much less rock and roll. Nevertheless, I come in on cue as Mike pounds out the intro. I am the only one who comes in on cue. Al actually forgets the words. To "Rock and Roll All Nite." There can't be more than twenty-five of them.

We stagger through "Black Diamond," "She," and "Detroit Rock City" before Al announces that he has to get home or his wife will kill him.

"This was awesome," Mike says. While I'm more than a little frustrated at how little this band sounds like the record, all of the old men are glowing.

"This is so much fun. Why the hell did we ever stop?" Stan says.

"Did it have to do with Ace stealing your girlfriend?" I offer.

"Shut up, Hank. You know what?" Stan says. "We should totally play Beachfest. Makeup and everything."

"People might mistake us for the actual band. You gentlemen are only slightly more portly than Gene Simmons himself!" I say.

They stare at me for a moment before cracking up. "Portly!" Al says. "That's good."

"We can practice here," Stan says. "Hank, are you game?"

"Only if we can call the band Music from The Elders," I say. Again my geriatric bandmates crack up.

"I like this kid, Stan," Mike says. "You're okay, kid. I like the fact that you're not afraid to bust our balls."

"Well, I got my own head busted earlier, so perhaps I have some residual anger," I say. This remark is completely serious, and it also cracks up The Elders.

Stan and I tidy up, and he drops me at home. I sneak in the door. Chase is not at home.

Mother is on the couch, asleep, with her wedding album open on her chest. An empty goblet of wine sits next to a two-thirds empty bottle of Merlot on the coffee table. I put the goblet in the sink, gingerly remove the wedding album, close it without looking, and replace it on the shelf. Even though it's summer, I find a blanket and cover Mother with it before going to my room.

CHAPTER 19
LIANA

At home, I peel my still-wet clothing off, wishing I could peel off the day too. All of it. The peaks and valleys my heart dealt with upon seeing my past, shirtless. The work I didn't do. My father's fifty-millionth round of tests. The party. But mainly Hank's stupidity. His lack of social grace. His complete inability to function without humiliating me.

I hang my shirt up in the bathroom, and when I wriggle out of my wet shorts I remove my wallet. The case is meant to be airtight, but I'm not sure that means waterproof. I open it to find three singles, one five, and a ten all damp and stuck together. I lay them on the counter to dry, then, underneath, see the white slip of paper. The slut note, which I still haven't discarded. The shame of today floods back. All those boys, knowing, their mouths on mine. The scorn from the girls. I spread the note out gently, staring at the word.

With a hair dryer set on low, I blow the heat onto the papers, crisping the bills and thinking. Hank makes me feel split inside. Two Hanks; one from the porch, swirling with music, the other a complete and utter social disaster, insensitive and plain dumb— frantic and unable to relax today, then ruining everything with his inability to keep his mouth shut.

"Liana?" my mother shouts into my room. "Come in to see us when you're done, okay?"

I give an affirmative grunt, wondering what baked good I'll have to sample today. The papers begin to dry. I contemplate crumpling up the slut note, but I can't. It's somehow a part of me now. Like those kisses I remember. How Pren Stevens tasted like licorice. How the light from under the bleachers looked like meteor shafts. How I know that if I ever kiss anyone ever again, which at this point is light years away, I won't have to wonder if it's okay. I'll just know.

I fold my money into a wad and tuck the note in, wondering if even the things that slice you open, that prick at you in the dark quiet of your own safe room at night, are worth savoring somehow. If they need to be kept and remembered. This makes me think of Jenny's picture and how my mother's response when she saw it on the counter the other day wasn't to bring it back to the basement, but to pile it up with all the albums and liner notes and have me do it. "Don't you want to take this to the basement?" she'd asked, as though reminding me about a favor I'd promised. I did return the albums but I pocketed the photograph and slid it in my desk drawer.

I go to it now, bringing it with me as I try to find my parents. They aren't in the living room, and they're not in the kitchen. Baffled, I check outside, but the porch is vacant, save for ghosts of "Waterloo Sunset" and me and Hank. My heart sinks, thinking of how we can repair his damage. How can we get past that?

"Dad?" I shout out. I find them in my mother's home office, where they're eating biscotti and sorting through accordion files, the way they do at tax time. "Paying bills?" I ask.

Dad blanches. "No. Just, uh . . . tidying up." He locks eyes with my mother.

"Did you have fun?" she asks, a few crumbs landing on her desk as she bites. Instantly she swipes them up with a cloth. "Want a few cappuccino biscotti?"

Suddenly this strikes me as odd—not her cleaning or forcing baked goods at me, she does that all the time, but that they aren't rejoicing in dad being around, making elaborate dinner plans or barbecuing. They're just dunking the biscotti in tepid coffee, their quiet chatter creeping up my skin as quiet and as insidious as mold.

"Dad had more tests." My mother locates a paper and hands it to my father. She looks pained.

"But he's fine," I say, and reach for a biscuit to placate her. As always, I think. I browse around the room for something, anything—that inexplicable missing item you want but can't locate when you return from being out with friends and come home to . . . home. I eye the calendar that hangs by the door. Dad's meant to be home for exactly a whopping three whole days this month—and he's already been here for two. "When do you leave for Orlando?"

Dad's biscotti sits so long in the coffee that when he removes it and waits to bite it, the end plops off, splattering him with dark brown liquid. "Shit. Goddamn it!" He swipes at his shirt with a napkin. My dad is not a swearer. Never has been. My mother is prone to cringe-worthy substitutions like "phooey" and "shucks" and "darn it all," but I can tell sometimes that she wants to yell *fuck fuck fuck* like there's no tomorrow. Only, she never would. It's like she's always waiting, letting the words cook inside herself, until she finally perceives me as able to handle it.

"I'm sticking around here for a bit," Dad says, and leaves his biscotti to disintegrate on the saucer. "I can come to Beachfest with you!" He tries for a joke.

"Yeah, right," I say, but inside my stomach turns. Beachfest. It's around the corner. The sure sign that summer's on its way out. What will I do about Hank?

My mother won't look up from her paper shuffling. I feel the photograph in my hands, keep it pressed against my stomach.

"Liana?" My mother stops me as I'm making my way out. She's seen the photograph in my hands, I'm sure. My skin pricks with nerves. "Here." She stands up and hands me something. I look down. "A pamphlet?"

I don't know whether to laugh or to scream, feeling both on their way out when I read the title aloud: "SEX-press Yourself: Healthy Ways to Navigate the Changing Waters." "You're giving me this?" I ask in disbelief.

My mother looks at my father, but he just begs off, focusing on the mushy biscuit. "I just thought . . ." she starts.

"Never mind the really bad grammar—Dad—have you seen this? Here's a sentence: 'Sometimes two young people want to show one another their feelings.'" I look at my father. "*One another* means more than two people. They should have written *each other*. *Each other* is two."

My mother puts her hands on her hips and comes out from behind the desk so she's between my father and me.

I continue reading, "'*My body is for me.*' Yeah, okay."

"I saw the note," she says, even though we all know it by now. My father even nods.

I let the silence leak into the room, flood the spaces around us, the spaces that are usually filled with cookies or muffins or test results. So she saw the slut note. Everyone in the world has seen it now. Or heard about it. Then, when I'm good and ready, I speak. "You have my report cards taped on the fridge. You have my science reports practically framed in the living room."

"We're proud of you. Of your accomplish—" My dad starts.

"But what about the kisses? The hookups?" I ask, and my voice is choked, tears from the whole mess of a day coming to my eyes. "You can't hide those either. Because they're a part of me." I pause. "And just so you know—it wasn't sex, okay? I never slept with them." And that's true, but I can tell from my mother's face that she's not buying it. The proof is in my virginity, but I won't play that card. All I wanted was the mouth to mouth. That's what they were, the kisses—proof of life in some way.

They wait for me to say more, so I do. "Just because you think you know something about someone doesn't mean that thing defines them. One thing—one word—or whatever, can't really define you." I hand the pamphlet back to her, and she takes it, letting the paper wilt in her hand. I turn to my dad. "I'm sorry you have to be stuck here."

His hand flies up, grasping mine. "That's not how I meant it, Li. The specialist thinks—"

"I get it," I say, shaking my head. "You need more tests." Again. Again. Never ending. I stare at my mother, at the pamphlet, needing to correct her, but unable to do so after today's events. "Here." I thrust the photo of Jenny at my parents and watch as the surprise shows up on their faces.

"Why do you have that?" my dad asks, and reaches for it.

My mother pulls it from his hands. "She had it in the kitchen the other day. She was looking around in the basement too."

"*I* had it in the kitchen," I correct her grammar. "*I'm* right here. Don't speak about me in the third person." My parents stare at me but don't let the photograph go. They process, my mother's hands calm and steady as though she's measuring flour, my father wordless, until he mumbles something about needing to get up early.

"I'm going out," I say to them. To no one. To myself.

"But you just got home," my dad answers.

"I know," I say, suddenly realizing I won't be able to sleep until I correct the course with Hank. "But I have to do something."

* * *

In movies, people are always having these revelations outside. They'll be walking to some diner or passing happy people partying on New Year's Eve and suddenly realize the meaning of life, or how to solve their personal crises. They pick up the pace until they are virtually sprinting on a New York sidewalk/the Vegas Strip/a Saharan dune toward the thing—mostly a person—who somehow will be the recipient of their newfound wisdom. This isn't quite what happens to me when I to get the beach.

I park by Sam & Nate's, lingering by the faded postcards. They display the shoreline behind me, an aerial shot of town, the bow-shaped coastline, and the carousel by the pier. It's weird to look at postcards of your own town, like seeing yourself from behind in the mirror, a completely foreign perspective. How sometimes you aren't sure what you're looking at, or what it might mean to someone else. How even if you know someone—really know them, not just what they like but who they are—you still might screw up.

And this is when I feel that rumble, as though I'm one of those on-screen revelation-prone people. My stomach burns, my heart rolls onto its side, and I know I need to find Hank. The window at Sam & Nate's is dotted with sunblock fingerprints, swatted flies, gritty sand, but when I peer through, I see a head of shaggy hair, a face tilted to one side—Hank. I suck in the salty air, and head inside, to find him by the root beer. For a second I smile, wondering if maybe he was buying me a bottle, or just thinking about me.

My shoes scrape the sandy linoleum. The harsh lights

do nothing to illuminate; they only turn everything inside—the magazines, the Frisbees, the posters for Beachfest—all a murky shade of green.

"Hey," I say, and reach my hand out to Hank's jacket. It too is green—one I haven't seen before.

He turns around. But instead of Hank's lopsided grin, his eyes darting this way and back, I see Pren Stevens and his bemused mouth, his eyebrows raised in a question he doesn't have to ask. I bound away, pretending I just remembered what I came in for, over in aisle two. Pren and his buddies linger around the DnD energy drinks, no doubt about to mix them with something stronger once in the dunes, and I crouch down. Unfortunately, my chosen location leaves me with little to look at save for the boxes of Band-Aids and small packets of maxi pads. The woman on the cover of the Gentle Days box looks carefree, as though her period, or whatever else might plague her, is washed away by the ocean breezes, which send her hair cascading down her non-specific shoulders. I bet she's never been horrified by her friend at a party. Never been totally overwhelmed by embarrassment. The front door smacks shut, and I stand up, making sure that Pren is gone.

I grab a packet of Twizzlers for Hank, thinking of when we went to Sweet Nothings together, how he'd said "All I can offer you is licorice," and I'd said it sounded like a sad song. I feel tears threaten the corners of my eyes. What if all we were was a sad song? People who met, became friends, and then faded like old stars, those planets you can still see remnants of but that don't exist any longer. I leave three dollars on the counter, slide the Twizzlers into my back pocket, head outside, and wish harder than anything that Hank was right here. That he'd know what I think and how I feel. That he'd know that I forgive him.

I stare at the night-empty street, the trash cans that will soon overflow with Beachfest debris, the pathways that will soon be crowded with concertgoers, and because, of course, Hank isn't here, I begin to walk. Moving my legs, feeling myself connected to the earth, tethered, makes me walk faster. And when I think about Hank, about how relief will spread across his face like chords into the air, I go faster. Past the swimming beach, the pier, the planetarium. I think of Hank, of "Waterloo Sunset," his eyes, his hands moving on the guitar, how he knows instinctively how to move his fingers, where to press to get the right sound, but how he won't know that with people maybe ever. And that's okay. I get to his house, winded, excited, smiling. I glance up at the sky one time before ringing the doorbell. The clouds have covered what was left of the stars.

The doorbell sounds as I catch my breath. Instead of feeling small and insignificant, like I did crouched on the floor of Sam & Nate's, I feel big. Like I take up room. Maybe that's why revelatory scenes take place outside—as though we, the masses of cells that split and re-form—can become something. So that even though we can't reshape what happened before, we can accept it, and kick on from there. I ring the bell again, but when no one comes, I try the door, and it opens with hardly a push.

"Hello?" I say, softly at first, in case his mom's home,

and then once more, louder, in case Hank's playing music.

"Up here!" A muffled reply lures me upstairs.

This is it. With each stair I come closer to breaking my pattern. No bolting. Just moving forward. I check Hank's room, but it's empty. Instinctively, I go to Chase's room, knowing how much time Hank spends in there. This room, too, is vacant. I sigh, feeling my shoulders slouch. It's all buildup and no show. Like when I'd rented an observatory-level telescope to watch a meteor shower last winter, only unpredictable weather moved in and blocked any and all views.

"To what do I owe this honor?" Chase asks me from the doorway.

I put my hands in my pockets, feeling small again. The Twizzlers rustle in my jeans. "Have you seen Hank? I need to . . . I just wanted . . ." I search the floor and walls as though they can provide answers.

Chase nods. "I got ya. Rough day, huh?" He wrinkles his mouth in a show of understanding. I nod back.

"You saw it, right? I mean, I couldn't . . ."

Chase wipes his face on the blue towel in his hands and flings it onto his bed. Only then do I realize he's in his boxers and nothing else. I look away, suddenly fixated on my watch. "God, it's late. I didn't even realize."

I stare at the wall again, looking at one of the lame tin signs Chase has nailed over his bed. LINE FORMS HERE. With a big blush I notice I am directly in front of it. Chase notices me notice this, and cracks up. "Looks like you're next!"

"Ha-ha. Very funny." I start to relax when I remember

we're in this together, that Chase was witness to the scene at the party, that unlike Hank, he is capable of comprehending what it was like for me. I think of my tattoo, that colored skin hidden under my shirt; how I wish I could curl up that small. "You think I overreacted?"

Chase swipes his hands through his wet hair, the blond marigold-bright even in the dimly lit room. "He doesn't mean it, you know?"

I stare at an old photo of Hank, one of those school-issued five-by-sevens that comes in multiples of ten. Chase walks toward me. "All the kid liked was maps, right? Everything maps. And directions. Give the kid an atlas or a gas-station-quality road map and he was all set for a whole afternoon."

I cross my arms over my chest. "And now it's music."

"Pretty much right after Dad died, yeah." Chase sits on his bed, the photo of Hank face-up, still staring at us. "He just switched."

I swallow hard. Maps. Music. In the pamphlet my mother gave me I remember the list: *menus, buttons, glass doorknobs, computer games, bathrooms, Victorian parasols. The Asperger's mind can latch on to anything and find it fascinating and comforting. And then just as quickly, let go.* "So where is he anyway?" I turn my back to Chase and look in the hallway for signs of Hank. I stand like that for a while, then pivot. "Should I wait?"

Chase stands up. Without thinking about it, I walk back toward him. We're maybe a few feet apart, but I can feel heat radiating off his chest, see beads of water trickle from the back of his hair down his spine. "You might have to wait a long, long time," Chase says, and it comes out in an almost-whisper. When he stands up and leans closer to me, I can smell the liquor on his breath. I don't know what kind or when he consumed it, but it doesn't really matter. What matters is I look at him and think of how easy it is to be with him and tell him how his brother doesn't know what he's doing in a group, how I want it to be simple, but it isn't.

"You sticking around or what?" Chase asks. His feet are in between mine now; one of his hands finds the Twizzlers in my back pocket. My skin ripples when he takes the package out and tosses it on the floor. Confident I won't go anywhere, Chase asks again. "You think you can wait?"

But I can't. I can't wait right now. All the words I had to say to Hank come rushing out in one long, intense mouth-to-mouth kiss with Chase. Chase pulls my hips into his, palms the back of my head, and we kiss hard, the sting of whiskey or scotch or whatever it is on my tongue from his, and my lips respond as though I'm suddenly quenched. I drink it in, wrapping my arms around Chase's bare body, caught out in space where I know I can't be doing this, but knowing it's happening. And it keeps happening, our mouths together, until we are broken by the sound of a guitar being chucked onto the floor and Hank standing in the bedroom doorway, his face the saddest song.

CHAPTER 20
HANK

So this is what the end of the world looks like. No mushroom cloud, no four horsemen thundering through the sky. Just your girlfriend kissing your half-naked brother.

This sight is odd in that it hurts far more than the blows to the head I received earlier. I feel as if a young, vigorous Pete Townshend has decided to smash a Les Paul on my midsection. It is difficult to breathe, and I am nauseous again. Liana looks at me, tears beginning to form in her eyes. "Oh, Hank," she says. "It's not . . . I didn't . . ."

Miraculously, I find breath enough to whisper, "I hope you'll at least have the decency to run away now."

Liana opens her mouth as if to speak and then obediently runs from the house.

I turn to Chase, and the paralyzing, breathtaking sadness that filled my stomach only seconds ago is replaced by rage stronger and deadlier than anything I've ever felt. My heart pounds, my fists clench, and my conscious mind turns off just as surely as it does when I'm lost in a guitar instrumental. Chase stands there with a stupid half-grin on his face that he often uses when trying to convince Mother not to punish him for something. Since he is clad only in boxers, it's difficult for me to avoid noticing the fact that he has half an erection. An erection that was caused by Liana's warm softness pressing against him. An erection caused by the taste of Liana's saliva in his mouth, by the feel of her lips against his, by the kiss that should have been mine.

I master my anger and deliver a speech that will surely devastate Chase, convincing him of my nobility and his own degeneracy: "You have everything. Everything. You have the normalcy and the athletic ability and the endless parade of girlfriends, and the one thing I've ever had in my life that was not yours, that was better than anything you've ever had, you had to take from me. You hate me so much that you had to destroy my happiness just because it wasn't yours."

As I'm going over the speech in my mind, I hear a strange noise. Upon closer examination the noise appears to be coming from my mouth. I'm bellowing and shrieking and kicking wildly at Chase, who is crumpled on the ground in the fetal position after I apparently drove my fist into his testicles. I am doing this. I am not calmly delivering the guilt-inducing speech.

I feel hands on me, and I wish I could stop making that horrible sound.

Mother grabs me and shouts, "Jesus, Hank! What

are you doing? Stop! Stop it right now!"

At last the noise stops. I give Chase one more kick, and then I'm done. I'm really not myself. I'm a demon of burning rage. I am the fire demon. "'Stand for the Fire Demon,'" I say, and Mother looks at me like I'm completely insane.

"What? What the hell are you saying? Why won't you tell me what's going on?"

"'Stand for the Fire Demon' is a Roky Erickson song. It was produced by Stu Cook from CCR."

Mother looks at me again. "Hank! Who the hell cares! Why the hell are you trying to murder your brother?"

"Ask him," I say. "He knows. He knows what he did."

"Freak," Chase croaks out. "He needs a goddamn straitjacket. Freak!"

"And you need a twelve-step program and a conscience," I say. "Tomorrow I will no longer be in a violent fugue of rage, but you will still be a drunk who betrayed his only brother."

"Betrayed?" Mother says. "Will somebody please tell me what the hell is going on?"

"Perhaps Chase will explain himself. It's bad enough I had to see that—I can't bear to relive it by telling you the story. Good night, Mother."

I walk down the hall to my bedroom, and suddenly the prospect of sleeping on the same floor as Chase is hateful to me. I grab a blanket from my bed and head to the basement, where I am surrounded by guitars. I lie down on the cold floor and do not sleep.

My phone rings. I look at the screen, though I know who

it is. "Liana" it says. I push a button to silence the ringer and turn over.

I fail to sleep, and I check the time. 1:17 a.m. 2:01 a.m. 2:30 a.m. It goes on like this, though there is a jump between 5:53 a.m. and 8:20 a.m. during which time I suppose I was asleep.

I get up and leave the house. I sit on the beach for an hour, trying and not succeeding to not think about Liana. The shock and anger of last night has turned to sadness and self-loathing. I wish I could reclaim the anger. Anger at least is a powerful emotion. Sitting here on the damp sand, feeling sad, I don't feel like someone who finally got the best of his older brother, I don't feel fearsome or strong, I just feel pathetic.

I hate myself for deluding myself. For believing that Liana and I could ever be more than friends. She is a girl. Girls prefer Chase to me. All girls. Always. Those who enforce the code of conformity in my school are given to calling me a number of creative variations on "homosexual." This morning, I am wishing they were right. Girls prefer Chase, but guys might not. I personally find him repugnant.

I get up and walk to Planet Guitar. Though we're not scheduled to open till 10 a.m., the door is open now, at 9:45. I enter the store and am greeted by the unmistakable sound of KISS's "Black Diamond" as being pounded out by three middle-aged men without a lead guitarist.

"Oh, thank God you're here. I called you like three times!" Stan says. "Why aren't you answering your phone? Jesus, you look like hell. Did you sleep outside?"

"To answer your questions in order," I respond, "one, I have not been answering my phone because someone I do not wish to speak with has been calling me."

"Girlfriend!" Al bellows at me, pointing and laughing. I give him a glare I hope is withering. "Geez, kid, lighten up," he says. "You called me portly last night. You can't dish it out like that if you can't take it."

"Fair enough," I reply. "You may now have some time to tease me about the fact that I caught my girlfriend kissing my brother." I am sincere in this offer, as Al's argument was logical and convincing. But my declaration is met only with silence.

"Oh. Oh, I'm sorry," Al says.

"Thank God he wasn't in the band," Stan adds. Mike, the drummer, is silent. I'm told this is characteristic of drummers, with the obvious exception of Keith Moon. "So, uh," Stan says, "did you kill him?"

"No, and I am actually relieved about that. I actually felt somewhat bad after punching him as hard as I could in the testicles"—all three of the men reflexively wince as I say this—"and kicking him while he lay on the ground."

"He deserved it," Mike says. "So are you ready to rock, or what?"

"I am always ready to rock, provided that Stan is willing to supply the equipment."

"I got you covered," Stan says. "Now, if we're going to play Beachfest at the end of the week, we've got to practice our asses off."

"But what of you gentlemen?" I say to Mike and Al.

"Surely you haven't been able to eat yourselves into that shape without working. Do you not have jobs to go to?"

Al looks at me for a long moment before smiling. "We took a couple of days off. The good thing about being old and portly is that either you own the store or you have enough juice in whatever organization you happen to be in that you can take a couple of days off on short notice. So when your good looks are gone, just hope you've worked enough to accrue some seniority."

I am puzzled by Al's reference to my good looks. I wonder if he's being sarcastic. I decide not to pursue the point any further.

Stan hands me a Les Paul, and I spend the next several hours as Ace Frehley. Today I like it better than being me.

CHAPTER 21
LIANA

I wrap my arms around my body as though I can hug myself. The air is colder now, hinting at fall's looming presence, but I only know it's cold because I have the chills from being kicked out. For once, I wanted to stay. For once, I knew what to do, what to say. I wanted to slam Chase and the me that kissed him back, ram both of us out of the way and rush over to Hank. To grab his hand and have him chord into mine.

Yet again I went for the easy thing. The kiss. And never got to the other stuff. So while it's beachside chilly now, I don't feel the air. All I feel is my kiss-swollen lips, my mouth—just the open space where words should be, not tongues.

I drive the way you're not supposed to—way emotional and with blurred vision due to tears that refuse to fall—but I know the roads well and skip a coffee in town in favor of going home. For once, what I want to do is tell my parents what happened. Some of it, anyway. Actually, what I want to do is tell Hank, but due to the fact that he is one of the parties involved, I can't. And Cat's away. And the lab's locked, so I can't lose myself in outer space. Like it or not my parents are last on the list.

The glass door slides open and I'm prepared to breathe in through my nose to sniff up whatever my mom's got in the oven. I wonder suddenly if Jenny were alive, if she'd lived somehow, if she'd be the one I'd go to now, tap gently on her bedroom door, and sit on the edge of her bed. If she'd listen. If she'd understand. Jenny's absence has never really felt like one, I guess. As I come into the kitchen's half-light and there's no scent—no honey whole wheat bread or caramel-chip cookies and no phone ringing and no ambient clatter that makes you know someone's awake and waiting for you—in the quiet, I miss her.

I check for signs of life in my parents' office, but it's dark. Their bedroom door is closed so I do a soft knock to see if they're awake, if Dad's watching late news or checking weather for his flight out.

"Hello?" I swing the door open. A wash of worry moves over me when I find their bed, bathroom, study, vacant.

I take the stairs two at a time and head back to the scent-less kitchen. Sure enough, there's a one-word note:

Hospital.

They've never left a note before. Never had a need. The trips to the ER have been casual, almost, and we've gone together or texted and said "no big deal" as a disclaimer. Zooming through traffic lights and swerving left on a no-left turn, my heart flares as loud as the ambulance sirens outside Westwood-Cranston. I jump out of the car and slam the door shut, still clutching my mother's note in my right hand. One word. She even put a period at the end as though it were a whole sentence. My shoes echo on the smooth emergency room floor. Maybe *hospital* is a whole sentence, a story—beginning, middle, and end. Just like my other note.

"Mom!" I run to where she stands, brows furrowed, half hidden behind a curtain. Before I can hug her I turn to look for my dad—draped in a gown as per usual—but the hospital gurney is empty. Just wrinkled sheets are left. I start to cry. "What happ . . . Oh my God!"

My mother puts her hands firmly on my shoulders, makes me look in her eyes. "He's okay. Or . . . he will be." Her eyes are puffy from crying, and her forehead is deeply creased with worry.

"It's not just tests?" I swallow hard, my pulse's velocity hitting overdrive.

She shakes her head and leads me to the empty bed, where I sit down. But I feel as though I'm sitting on a sickbed, a bed where my healthy but neurotic father should be, so I stand up. "Tell me what's going on."

We leave the eerie bodiless bedroom and sit in the waiting area with other hushed and sad people. My mother sips water from a Styrofoam cup that squeaks when she puts it to her lips. "Here." She hands me the cup even though I haven't asked.

I take a sip of tepid water, watching my mother's chest rise and fall rapidly, her own quick breathing matching mine. "So tell me already," I say, because the suspense only makes me more frantic.

"He's in surgery. But wait—before that—we were sitting there and he went very pale and—" My mother is calm as she says this.

"He was really sick," I say, and think back to their conversation in the study. How my father had said he wasn't leaving so soon. My mother puts her hand on my forearm, her palms cool. "Those last tests, they were for real." She watches my face.

"I can't believe this!" I try to keep my voice down, but I can't. No one else in the family waiting area seems to care. Probably there've been huge fights, sobs, tears of relief here. I am not the first.

"You guys should've told me. Outright. Not hinted. What does it take, a pamphlet?" I stare at the patterns on the floor. "Do you know how many boys I've kissed?" Now I stare at her. She waits, every part of her dreading a double-digit number I don't deliver. "But do you know why?" I sigh and wipe the tears off my face, thinking of Hank. Of his eyes when he saw me with Chase. "Because I can't talk . . . I don't speak enough . . ." I stop short. My mother waits. She'll keep waiting, I think, maybe for as long as I need, so I say, "It's not like it's totally your fault, or mine. Sometime I'll tell you more, okay?" Instead of yelling, instead of freaking out and hushing me into acceptable quiet, my mother scoots her chair toward me and hugs me hard. We both cry for a while.

Then she explains. "After she died, we just . . . we stopped talking about it. We did just what you're not supposed to do. And I should know. I'm the expert, right? I give advice about this sort of thing every week. But it's not the same when it happens to you. Other people's issues—their patterns—always seem easy to break, to conquer."

Patterns, people. I flash to Hank chording, his staccato speech, the social flinching. I thought I could cure him. Change him. Morph him enough that he wouldn't say the wrong thing or do it. Or not do it. And I thought I could snap myself out of my own kiss-induced stupor with a simple pact. No kissing. Like that solved anything. My mother looks up as a doctor in seawater-blue scrubs passes by. No news for us yet. "And when Dad was home, he'd feel . . . I don't know. Palpitations. Stress. But he couldn't see that it wasn't . . ."

"Like when you don't say what you need to, or you don't delve into the reasons behind things . . . you just fix the symptom, not the issue," I say. *Please let him be okay. Please.*

My mother gives me a wry smile. She looks at another physician, but the surgeon goes to another family. My mother's eyes well up. "Sometimes it's hard to tell what's a symptom of grief and what's . . ."

"Real?" How do you know what you feel versus what you want to feel? How can you be sure that what you're looking at—a star, a planet, a face—is what you truly see? I think about the planetarium with Hank. How I knew. How I could say anything to him but kept clinging to the slip of paper in my wallet as my defense.

Before I can say anything else, a woman, with a mask on her face and what looks to be a shower cap on her head, emerges from the double doors and spots my mother. The whole world seems to lose oxygen; my chest is weighted, heavy with anticipation. My mother grabs my hand.

"My dad?" I ask, and leave my mouth hanging open. I picture my dad's hands, how they taught me to look into a telescope. How he sliced his thumb on a deck nail and got stitches. How he shoves his work into his briefcase and then it doesn't close properly. How he smiled when he saw me parallel park for the first time. How he frowned when he saw how I did it the second time—half on the curb. How he always messes up the words to "Solsbury Hill," that Peter Gabriel song neither of us understands. How he looked in his hospital bed at the beginning of the summer. How much has changed since then.

"He's going to be fine. The Maze surgery seems to have gone well." The doctor turns to me and starts to explain. "Any irregularity in your heart's natural rhythm is called an arrhythmia. Presumably you know your dad had an arrhythmia—it was treated with medicine." My mother nods, looking at me.

"It didn't work, apparently," my mother says, and still keeps my hand in hers. "They did this . . . Maze surgery suddenly, Liana. But they would have had to do it anyway. It was scheduled for next week."

I feel punched. "That's why Dad changed his flights?"

The doctor coughs. "Flying carries with it an increased risk of stroke—blood clots—"

"So you knew he'd need heart surgery and didn't say anything?"

"We tried to." My mother drops my hand and smoothes her hair, keeping calm. "But you left so quickly tonight."

The next morning is still really part of the night before since I never went to bed. I arrive back in the cardiac care unit and join my mother in my dad's room. I place her change of clothes and bathroom bag on the chair by the window.

"Thanks," she says. Outside, the late summer morning light ripples over the parking lot and, farther on, the water.

I stare at my dad, at the familiar sight of him in a hospital gown, but this time with the jarring additions of tubes and monitors, his skin slightly pasty.

"Dad." Gingerly I touch his hand.

"It's okay," my mom urges.

I sit with him, pulling my T-shirt over my tattoo. He knows it's there, probably, but why flaunt it now? Dad's himself—that is, able to talk and look at me—just tired. "How you holding up?" he asks.

"Me? How about you?"

"So many pronouns," he offers.

I shake my head. "I have a cell phone, you know." I display it. "Next time—maybe call me when you guys are experiencing life-changing things."

"*Things . . . Things* is nonspecific. Say 'events.'"

"God, Dad. Way to ruin a moment," I joke, and touch the scar on his thumb from when that deck nail sliced him.

"There won't be a next time," Dad assures me.

We sit there for a while, talking, not talking, my mother and I take turns resting or going to the cafeteria. I return to the vending machine and think of Hank and his M&M's, how small events—him showing up in the bathroom, say—can change everything. And how big ones—my dad's emergent heart surgery—can stabilize your world. How nothing, but everything, has changed. How I don't look it, but I feel it in my skin. Like I could check my tattoo to find that the planets have tilted or vanished. And how really, all the bright objects we see from Earth aren't there anymore—stars aren't what we make them to be—they're already burned, faded, remnants of what was. The half-life. How I need to tell Hank all of this, but how I suspect he won't let me even try.

CHAPTER 22
HANK

Eventually the day has to end. Al, Mike, and Stan have to go back to their families, and I have to go . . . where? Espresso Love? Tainted. Forever tainted. Perhaps there is a lesson here about whether one should take one's girlfriend to one's favorite places. Then when said girlfriend reveals herself to be perfidious, you've lost your favorite places and your girlfriend.

The dream of having a girlfriend is dead, and so is my backup dream. If it hadn't been for Liana, I would have been able to purchase the Jazzmaster by the end of the summer. As it is, I now have a cell phone and no one I have any desire to talk to. And the Jazzmaster mocks me silently from the wall, reminding me of playing it for a girl I thought cared about me. Even if I could afford it now, I wouldn't want it. It would only remind me of dashed hopes, of betrayal. I walk out of Planet Guitar and onto the sidewalk.

The sun is still shining, but beach time is over. Bikini-clad girls with pierced navels walk down the sidewalk, their flip-flops slapping the concrete. They giggle and point at shirtless knuckle-dragging troglodytes, and I remember Joe Jackson singing about pretty women out walking with gorillas.

I have no place to go and no one to go there with. So I walk.

Eventually I take my phone from my pocket to see what time it is. This is not really important information except that Chase is usually out of the house by eight, and I do not want to be in the house before then. "Six New Voice Messages," my phone announces.

I do not want to listen to the messages, but I call the voice mail number anyway. I occasionally get zits in my ear. Perhaps because the skin there is not very elastic, these particular zits are very painful. And it's especially painful to pop them. And yet I always do it, knowing it's going to be painful, because it is satisfying, in a disgusting way, and when the zit is in your ear, you can actually hear it pop, which is interesting. I suspect I'm listening to my voice mails now for a similar reason.

First new message. "Hey, it's Stan. Sorry to call so late, but I just got off the phone with Mike—" DELETE.

Second new message. "Hank. It's Liana. I—" DELETE.

Third new message. "Hey. Me again. I really need to talk to you. There's a lot of—" DELETE.

Fourth new message. "Hank. Stan again. Sorry to call so early. I'm just wondering—" DELETE.

Fifth new message. "Hank? Come on . . . it's Liana."

She sighs for a long time. "I'm back at the hospital with my dad." I feel it would be wrong to hang up with that news. "He's okay. I think it's all okay. But I need to . . . It's just that I . . . Maybe this won't even make sense to you, but I just—I was really scared, okay?" Another sigh and a kind of laugh. "Did you know when an astronaut goes into space their body changes? Like everything up there causes the astronaut to feel different . . . even look kind of different. This is probably really boring to you, but I'm just gonna keep talking because you're probably not even listening anyway. I mean, you deleted me already, right?" I swallow and shake my head at my phone. She goes on. "So, the human body's like this integrated system, you know? All the parts talk to the other parts. And they depend on the parts to communicate. You probably know that already. Anyway, on Earth, bodies have an *Earth-normal* condition. The usual way of being. But in space, the system changes. That's *space-normal*." I look at the phone. She's lost me in the astronomy. "The thing is, Hank, you're my space-normal condition. Or, I mean, you're how I want to be. Or how I am now. Maybe I was scared of how I feel about you, afraid about changing. But the kissing part—that was the old me, and it's not like I'll ever get rid of that person, because they're always in you. Like we see stars but we're not seeing them for real, just the outline of what they were. So I just fell into my old pattern, kissing somebody—that'd be Chase, who's kind of, how to say, a douche? I kissed someone I don't really like and don't care about when I should have been telling you all this instead." She takes a big breath. "That's all."

Sixth new message. "Hey. Stan. Forgot to tell you to come in early again tomorrow. Bye." DELETE.

I replay Liana's message several times as I walk. I try to understand the astronaut stuff. I wonder briefly if this is how other people feel when I go on at length about some topic, such as the instrumentation of Love's "Forever Changes," that is endlessly interesting to me but perhaps less so to them. I understand that Liana is talking in metaphors, though. And what she is telling me is that she prefers me and regrets kissing Chase. Liana does not care about Chase and doesn't like him. She believes him to be a douche. Insofar as a douche is something that is useless at best but that some women put into their bodies anyway, I believe her description of Chase to be wholly accurate.

I no longer know how to feel. My anger was pure and powerful. My sadness was deep and dark. I don't know if there's a name for what I feel now, except perhaps for confused. Was this something that was to be expected? It is only seven thirty, but I am hungry and tired of walking. I stop at White's Market and buy peanut butter and Marshmallow Fluff and whole wheat bread. I am going to make myself a sandwich that happens to have been my father's favorite. I miss him very powerfully tonight. This is a situation that calls for a father, or so movies and television shows would have me believe. "Dad," the teen son says, "I just don't understand girls."

And the dad looks around guiltily, making sure the mom is not within earshot, and says, "Nobody does, son. Nobody does."

I don't have a father. I have only his sandwich. It'll have to do.

I walk into the house and find Mother seated at the kitchen table. "Hey," she says.

"Hello, Mother," I say, and I unpack my bag of food on the table in front of her. She looks at it for a moment and then says, "I miss him too. God, I miss him so much today."

I grab a knife and a plate and make myself a sandwich. "Would you like one?" I ask.

"Sure," she says.

I make the sandwich, and we sit and chew in silence for a moment. "So you may have noticed that Chase isn't here," Mother says. I don't say anything. "He's at Nana's." I still don't say anything, but I suppose the shock is evident on my face. "Well, not really. I thought you guys could use a break from each other, and Papa is actually going on a three-day sail, so Chase is currently crewing Papa's boat."

"With any luck, he'll drown," I say.

"You know . . . well, I can't say I blame you for feeling that way. But we . . . Does it make an impression on you that I called them for help?"

"It is uncharacteristic behavior on your part," I offer.

"Damn right it is. But we're . . . we're broken, Hank. Our family. We're all we have, and we're broken, and I couldn't fix it by myself."

I have nothing to say to this.

"So I'm hoping that three days at sea with no booze will help your brother come to terms with what he's becoming. He's not really—he's a sweet boy under it all, he really is.

He's just got a problem. Possibly a couple of problems. Hell, we all do."

"I, for example, have a douche for a brother and a perfidious girlfriend."

Mother looks at me for a moment. Then she continues. "And I can't understand why I can't keep living a life that ended five years ago."

I don't fully understand what this means, only that it has something to do with my father, and, apart from eating the sandwich, that's a subject I do not wish to pursue any further. I decide to change the subject before Mother goes too far down that road. "Mother. I wonder if you can help me understand something."

"I can certainly try."

"I received voice mails from Liana."

"I'm sure she feels terrible."

"As well she should. But I have . . . she said, if I understand her lengthy astronaut metaphor correctly, which I suppose is a big if, that she was afraid of becoming someone new and so she fell back on the pattern of who she was. Does this make any sense to you?"

"Oh God, does it ever."

"Can you explain it?"

"I don't know, Hank. I mean, it's just . . . I mean, your father was . . . well, I hadn't dated anyone like him, and then, you know, I found myself pregnant with your brother, and there I was, this punk rock chick who was pretty much defining herself by being young and irresponsible, and I had to face the prospect of growing up and being responsible. I mean,

I wasn't happy being young and irresponsible, not really, but it was an unhappiness I understood and was familiar with, and it was terrifying to think of letting it go."

"I don't think I can understand that."

"I think you probably can. But, listen. I'm going to tell you a secret. I need you to never tell another soul—not Nana, not Chase, not Liana, not Stan, not anyone. Ever. Can you agree to that condition?"

Mother is familiar enough with the way I am that she understands the need for total clarity in situations like this. "I agree."

"If you ever break this promise, Hank, it will cause a rift between us that will never be fully repaired."

"I understand."

"I went and scheduled—your father and I had a huge screaming fight about it because he was determined to have the baby, but I scheduled an abortion anyway and went to the clinic alone and sat in the waiting room. And then I went running back to your father in tears, telling him how I couldn't go through with it, and I wanted to have the baby and raise it with him. And I told him . . . I told him how sorry I was, and how scared I'd been. And do you know what he did?"

"He forgave you."

"Yes. And if he hadn't, you would never have existed. I would have raised Chase on my own, and possibly found someone else or not, but *you* might not ever have walked the earth. That's how powerful it is to forgive someone, Hank. Your whole existence hung on that one act of forgiveness."

"I will chew on that, Mother, metaphorically speaking. Literally speaking, I will chew on another sandwich. Will you join me?"

"Nah. One's my limit. Do you want to watch some TV or something?"

"I don't think so. But thank you. I barely slept last night, and I'm feeling quite exhausted."

"You'll probably sleep better in your bed than on the basement floor. I'm just saying."

I decide Mother is right. I go to my room and lie in my bed. And despite my fatigue, I do not fall asleep. An hour and a half later, I wander downstairs for a drink of water and find Mother in front of the computer. She snaps it shut, but not before I see that the site she is on is widowdate.com. I get my glass of water and return to my room without comment. I cannot imagine what about the scene she witnessed last night made Mother think it was time for her to start dating again, but I've become reconciled to the fact that there are many things I will simply never understand.

Another day without Liana. Another day immersed in the work of KISS. Al is excited because he has a line on some costumes, and Mike's wife can do very credible KISS makeup, to judge by the Peter Criss cat face she painted on Mike this morning.

We practice all day, and I don't think about Chase or Liana or really anything except for the pyrotechnics issue: Al is keen to attach Roman candles to the back of the necks of the guitars and bass, and shower the crowd with sparks during our finale performance of "Rock and Roll All Nite," while Stan is understandably reluctant to subject his merchandise to the whims of amateur pyrotechnics.

I find their argument amusing, and without thinking, I find myself wanting to call Liana to tell her about it.

This, I realize as I'm walking home (sure of Chase's absence, I'm content to walk home directly from work), means that I've already made the decision to forgive her. I miss her. As far as she is from understanding me (and, it must be said, I'm at least that far from understanding her), Liana is one of the few people who seems even remotely close to understanding me, and certainly one of very few who like me because of the way I am rather than in spite of it.

I don't know if it will be torturous to hang around with her if she doesn't consider me boyfriend material. How will I react when she tells me she's dating the greatest guy? That will be horrible, but missing her all the time is horrible too.

Here is the problem: I don't know how to have a delicate conversation. And I suspect that "I forgive you for kissing my brother, and I would like to be your boyfriend, but I'll settle for being just your friend even though that would be torture to me, because I don't want to live without you anymore, and oh yeah, how is your hospitalized father" probably qualifies as a delicate conversation. And I'm sure I will screw it up somehow and lose her again.

Distracted, I microwave something from the freezer, and after two minutes, I have to check to make sure I've been eating the entree and not the box.

Mother returns home from work, says hello, and checks

her e-mail. She smiles broadly and snaps the laptop closed. I like seeing her smile.

I know what I have to do. And I know how to do it. My phone proves useful after all, and I'm glad I didn't throw it away the other night. I send a new text message to Liana's phone: "Beachfest promises to be interesting."

CHAPTER 23
LIANA

By now I'm used to the noises and smells of my dad's room. He'll be in the ICU for another few days, then the regular ward for another five. Then home to recover for the next couple months.

"No flying for me," he says, patting the edge of the bed so I'll sit with him.

"Just as well," I say, and feel my back pocket for my wallet. It presses against me, and I take it out, uncomfortable.

"Because of blood clots?" he asks.

"No," I tell him directly. "Because then you're home. With us."

His eyes flutter closed, but he smiles. My mother shoos me out of the room and follows me, eyeing the wallet in my hands. "Do you need any money?" she asks. I shake my head. "That's"—she points to the case—"a bit bulky, don't you think?"

I can see the edges of the note inside. "I guess I'm used to it," I say, and then wonder if maybe that's her point.

My mother nods to a nurse walking by. "I think I'll try to watch a bit of TV while he rests. *A Star Is Born*. Great film," she says. "Are you heading home?"

"Not yet. I have to finish up at the lab." I check my watch.

"I don't suppose you want to stay."

"For *A Star Is Born*?" I shake my head. "Stars are born from interstellar gas clouds, shine by nuclear fusion, and then die, sometimes in dramatic ways." We lock eyes and then smile.

"Liana?" My mother pulls something from her purse. "I thought you might want to hang this up at home. In the hallway."

She hands me the picture of Jenny I found in the basement with Hank. I hold it to my chest and nod. "Sure." I check my watch again. "I gotta run to the lab—but I'll be back tonight."

My mother furrows her brows. My stomach clutches when I think she's reconsidering the photo. But when she reaches for me, it's not for Jenny's picture. It's for my face. She touches my cheek, and I don't shrug her off. "Don't come back tonight."

"But I—you don't want me here?" I've gotten used to it here, to talking with them, to the confines and safety of my father's hospital room.

"You shouldn't be here. You have Beachfest."

Hearing the word from my mother's lips sounds awkward—like hearing your parents swear or attempt slang. "Beachfest's . . ." I stumble over words. "Nothing. No big— It's—I'm not going." I think about Hank in the hospital bathroom. About him in Espresso Love. About him playing there. About him onstage. About him anywhere. "I can't go to Beachfest." *Beachfest promises to be interesting.* Interesting in that way when you pick a scab: half-fascination, half-wincing dread. Seeing Hank there—or not—will only remind me of my mistakes. Of what could have been.

"Of course you can."

"But Dad's . . ."

"Dad's fine." She pauses and looks me up and down. "It's you that needs help." She studies my wallet again.

"What's that supposed to mean?"

"Just go. Have fun. Or try to at least." I turn to go, and she pivots back into Dad's room. "And, Liana?" I figure she'll tell me not to mess around with anyone. Or not to wind up in the basement with anyone. Or not to do something. But all she says is, "Maybe think about changing? You reek of hospital."

But I do wind up in the basement. I hand in my report, close up the lab for the rest of the summer, knowing full well I'll be back in there again when school resumes, and head home. To the basement. I trudge down there and haul the turntable back up. This time to my room, and connect the speakers. I take the picture of Jenny from my bag and slide it into a frame and put it up in the hallway right near our other family shots—vacations, moments, times passed that still shine on. I bring an armful of records up with me, the ones Hank pointed out, and I listen as I get ready. I can't put on "Waterloo Sunset" because that will make me upset. I rewind and replay in my mind the text Hank sent, "Beachfest promises to be interesting." *Beachfest Promises* almost sounds like the title of an album—one with some cheesy sunset and 1970's era couple in luau shirts or something. I shouldn't go. I should stay here.

I put the albums in a stack on my desk and look at The Kinks. I don't play it. But I put on The Band and listen to "Stagefright" and "The Weight," and the twangy bango reverbs into the pre-fall air, and I think about starting over again like they say in the song, and how that's what everyone has to do every day, and I slide into my comfiest jeans, tug my old Squeeze T-shirt over my tattoo, and slide on flip-flops to combat the sand at Beachfest.

CHAPTER 24
HANK

My hair is short, so I'm wearing a wig. My face is covered in makeup. I am wearing a skintight black body suit with silver accents and silver platform boots.

Al, stuffed like a sausage into his Gene Simmons costume, is breathing deeply and pacing around backstage in his giant, toothsome platform boots. "Wow. I mean. Wow. I had no idea I'd be this nervous. I mean, this crowd is mostly teenagers, right? The cruelest, most brutal people on earth. No offense, Hank."

"None taken," I say. "Your remark is wholly consistent with my own experience."

Al smiles at me, and I decide to make a joke. Al likes it when I make jokes at his expense. "I was wondering," I say, "if the mirrored codpiece is as uncomfortable as the rest of your costume, or if you have more room in that area."

"The mirrored—"

"Codpiece. The piece which covers your—"

"Shortcomings!" Stan chimes in.

Al reaches down to his crotch, adjusts the mirrored codpiece, and says, "No. This thing is killing Al Junior. First time in my life I wish I was more like Stan."

Stan smiles through his Paul Stanley makeup.

Onstage, two white boys in baggy basketball jerseys, baseball caps, puffy basketball shoes, and large gold necklaces prance around the stage to pre-recorded music and nearly swallow their mikes as they boast of their rhyming prowess and instruct the crowd to throw their hands in the air.

"Hank, you're young. Does this suck as much as I think it does?" Stan asks, pointing a thumb at the stage.

"Well, their rhyming prowess is far below the level of their boasting, but, on the other hand, the beat they are rapping over samples the bass intro from Cream's 'Badge,' combined with the horn break from an Otis Redding song I'm having a hard time identifying, so they at least have a talented producer."

The other members of Music from the Elders stare at me briefly, then go back to their preperformance rituals. I have no ritual. I do not feel nervous, at least not about the Music from the Elders part.

The white rappers leave the stage and strut around the backstage area, making ambiguous hand signals and screaming, "Yeah! What? What?"

The MC, a bikini-clad college student, takes the mike,

ignores the insistent calls from the crowd to remove her top, and says, "And now, ladies and gentlemen, give a big Beach-fest welcome to . . . Music from the Elders!"

"Ready for a surprise?" Mike says from behind his Peter Criss makeup as we take the stage.

"What? What did you do?" Stan and Al gibber at him.

"No time to talk. It's time to rock!" Mike says, grinning.

He sits behind the drum kit, and the rest of us clomp to the front of the stage. I am relieved that I don't fall. Walking in six-inch platform boots is actually quite challenging. I plug in my Les Paul and survey the crowd—a sweaty, cheering, at least partially drunk sea of humanity with no idea who I am. I'm anonymous and very, very tall.

"Here we go," Mike says, and clicks his sticks together four times.

Simultaneously, Stan, Mike, and I rip into the intro to "Detroit Rock City." The intro to this particular song repeats, and just before the repetition of the intro, flash pots on either side of the stage give off a loud BOOM and send up fire and smoke. I can hear Al laughing at Mike's surprise, and he steps to the mike and begins to sing.

The crowd goes insane. And, ultimately, why wouldn't they? Our band sounds great and looks—well, if not great, at least visually interesting. And we have pyrotechnics. We have come to slay them with the power of our rock, and they thank us for it.

"Detroit Rock City" ends, and I grab the acoustic guitar to play the intro to "Black Diamond."

When Al shouts out "Hit it!" signaling the song's transition from acoustic to electric, the flash pots go again, and we all send glances of affectionate annoyance at Mike, who is lost in his drumming.

"Black Diamond" segues directly into the thumping tom-tom intro to "Rock and Roll All Nite." During the no-guitar part of the song, I do what people in my position do during such passages. I step to the front of the stage and clap my hands over my head, and the crowd follows suit as if playing a colossal game of Simon Says in which I'm Simon.

I take a moment to scan the crowd for familiar faces, which is to say I look for Liana. I spot Mother and Chase, both smiling and clapping, and then, at the far edge of the crowd, I see the person who isn't clapping over her head, but rather, nodding her head slightly. It's Liana.

Now I'm nervous.

Fortunately, the rest of the band had decided that what "Rock and Roll All Nite" really needed was a guitar solo. I argued unsuccessfully against this in rehearsal, pointing out that the song's lack of a solo is part of its magic, and furthermore, that it prefigured punk rock, and so it would be not only inaccurate but perhaps historically misleading to insert a solo into the song.

The rest of the band insisted, and now I am glad for it as I stride to the front of the stage and pour all my fear and hope and love into the Les Paul, and what comes out is a solo I hope Ace Frehley would be proud of.

The song ends with the third and final burst of the now-spent flash pots, and we all stand and bow. The other members of Music from the Elders exit the stage, and Stan, my accomplice, throws me two towels from the wings. I walk to the mike at the front of the stage, as terrified now as I was confident just a moment ago. My instinct is to run, to just revel in my moment of triumph before I undoubtedly humiliate myself. But I've planned out some rock-and-roll showmanship, and I am going to stick to the plan.

"As you all know, the real members of KISS wore makeup not only for purposes of showmanship, but also to conceal the fact that they are very ugly men." The crowd gives a few confused cheers.

"Fortunately, I have no such problem." I take off my wig and throw it into the crowd. I grab the towel with cold cream on it and vigorously rub my face. I grab the plain towel and wipe the residue off my face. I'm sure my face is still streaked with makeup, but I'm also pretty sure it's now clear who I am. I look into the crowd and find Liana. She's grinning. Yes. It is clear that it's me.

"Another difference between us is that KISS wrote songs for money. I wrote this one for love," I say. The crowd cheers, and the rest of the band, still in KISS makeup, returns to the stage. Stan carries his Paul Stanley Washburn and a Fender Jazzmaster, which he places in my hands, but not before pointing out the modification on the neck.

Mike clicks his sticks together, and I play my intro, step to the mike, and say, "This song's called 'Planet of Love.'" Then I begin singing the song I wrote for Liana. It goes a little something like this:

I don't know what you're trying to Chase
Running around in outer space
Hoping to find the perfect place
But it's here, yeah it's here

I don't know what you hope to find
Watchin the Milky Way unwind
But you're outta my life, and I'm outta my mind
Over you . . . over you

Just come back, baby
Land on the planet of love

I don't know what you think you'll see
Zooming around the galaxy
When the atmosphere's right for you and me
Right here, right here

Just come back, baby
Land on the planet of love

By this point, a few interesting things have happened. For one, Liana and I locked eyes at the beginning of the song, and neither of us has looked anywhere else since. It is rather strange and, frankly, arousing, to be having this intimate moment in the midst of thousands of other people. I am relieved to have a guitar covering my spandex-clad crotch. Also, this is the point in the song at which I insert a blistering solo. Though the song is, musically speaking, a Cheap Trick pastiche,

241

my solo is not really in the style of Rick Nielsen. The crowd doesn't seem to mind. In fact, they cheer rather loudly. Then they cheer even louder when I trigger Mike's amateur pyrotechnics and sparks begin shooting out from the tube he's attached to the back of the neck. I see Liana laughing, and for a second I really wish I could silence the band and the crowd and everything but the sound of her laughing.

But I have one more verse and three repetitions of the chorus to get through. Which I do, I think. All I can think of is Liana.

The crowd cheers. They apparently don't mind the fact that the song doesn't have a bridge.

Liana cheers. She apparently doesn't mind the fact that the song casts her as a wayward interstellar traveler, when I was the one who kicked her out of the house and didn't answer her messages.

I can't stand being separated from her any longer. I assess the situation. I could probably stage dive and be passed over the heads of the crowd back to where Liana is standing, but I am frankly quite uncomfortable with that many people touching me, especially when I'm wearing skintight spandex.

I gingerly hop from the stage and find myself immersed in an appreciative crowd and unable to see Liana. Many people are touching me, but at least this is confined to the top half of my body.

A few people hug me as I make my way through the crowd, and then suddenly, someone is hugging me hard enough to make it difficult to breathe. My assailant releases me, and I realize it's Chase.

"Dude," he says. "You rock!"

I can't help smiling. Especially since the last thing he said to me was something to the effect that I am mentally ill. Remembering that I owe my existence to forgiveness, I look at him and say, "Thank you. I suppose, under the right circumstances, I do."

"Listen. I'm sorry. I was a total dick, and I—"

"Chase. I forgive you."

"Thank you, Hank. I do . . . I mean, I know I'm an idiot sometimes, but I really do, you know, love you."

"And I recognize that I may occasionally be difficult to live with, and I love you as well. And I am sorry for punching your testicles. But now I must seek out the girl I love. You understand."

"The funny thing is, I kind of don't. I mean, for all the girls I've . . . I mean, yeah, there have been a lot of girls, but as far as love, I mean, well, I guess I don't really—"

"Chase, this line of conversation sounds intriguing, but I really must go."

"Oh, yeah. Go. I'll catch you later."

Well, now I'm the one dismissing Chase for babbling, and I'm going to find a girl while he stands there alone. The world has truly turned upside down. Or it will, as soon as I find her.

CHAPTER 25
LIANA

The light shifts from late afternoon to early evening, and I slide out of my flip-flops to feel the cold sand on my feet. Music swells around the stages, the revelers, everyone outfitted in candy-colored tank tops and faded jeans. Some drink electric-blue frozen drinks from eco-friendly cups that read "Life's a Beachfest." One of many. I pull my wallet from my pocket, thinking I might purchase something, but find myself frozen, stuck staring at the note that has taken up residence. The four letters are faded, sure, but still there. I think about finding the note amid the detritus in my locker, how it fluttered to the ground shooting-star-like, how I picked it up and kept it all summer. I take it in my fingers now, amazed at how such a small thing, a lightweight slip, could have altered me so much. How the photograph of Jenny, which is only a bit larger, rocked my parents' world.

Rather than hanging it up, though, I take the note and half consider dropping it into the ocean as some ritualistic ode to my past. But I don't. I just slide it back into my wallet until it eventually finds its way into a box in the basement. I don't need to throw it out to know where it belongs.

I bypass the large stage, where Fortress of Smallitude belts out their one and only hit, mill around for a minute by the blue iced drink stand, but then find myself following a trail of people toward the side stage. I have no intention of listening to the music—I just want the view. But the beach is crowded, the throngs of concert-goers swaying as they walk, then clumping together, swaying and nodding to the sounds of some cover band. "Hey, these guys don't suck," someone says, and gestures to the stage with his blue drink. It sloshes onto my toes and I pause, wondering what to do next, but find I don't care about the cold sticky mess when I focus on the stage. It's not that the band sucks or doesn't. It's who is in it. I don't even mouth Hank's name when I see him, spandex-enrobed, playing for a larger audience than just Espresso Love. Bigger than just for me. I stand with my sticky foot and watch them finish their set, wishing not so much that I could flip back time and correct what I did or didn't do, but that I could linger here for a minute longer.

KISS filters out through the speakers, and I can't help but smile—at the songs, at the way people cheer for him, at his stunningly ridiculous makeup. The set ends, and I expect Hank to run off stage, free from the gaze of many, but he stays there, speaks into the microphone, and when he says "Planet of Love," I think I'm about to explode. Every bit of my body unfurls, and I am pulled to the words, the chords, to him.

Space helmets have three visors to adjust to changing light conditions. That's what I need now to contend not with the mellowing sunshine over the water, but the way the song ripples through my body. The way that Hank changed enough to write it—not just play a cover of someone else's song—and I changed enough to hear it and stay grounded in the sand.

The song ends, and Hank comes off the stage, wipes his face on a towel, and makes his way toward me. I don't move. I don't run to him or away from him. I just plant myself in the sand. He's closer now, close enough that I can see the white goop on his hairline, close enough that my heart pummels in my chest. It takes only ninety minutes to orbit through an entire day in space. That's how this summer feels—so fast, but just as expansive as space. That's the thing: space isn't empty. We use the word like that, but the truth is, space is cluttered with quarks and stars and dust and planets, just like our pasts are littered with loss or chords or hospitals or guitars or kisses or a lack of being able to say what we need to say.

So when Hank appears in front of me, sweat and stage makeup on him, his cheeks flushed with performance and revelations, I say, "I missed you."

"But I'm here," he says, and looks down. "You have a blue foot."

I swallow and reach for his hand. "The song . . ." I take a breath. "Yeah, you are here."

He grins. "And you're here."

I nod. "Still."

And because I'm not going anywhere, and neither is he, I lean into him. Our chests touch, and when his mouth is poised to meet mine, I don't back away. I put his hand on my tattoo, not to cover it, but so he can see it. With his thumb pressed into it, my skin feels new almost. Hank doesn't interrupt the moment to tell me that Ace was an art student and designed the KISS logo, or that Brian May, Queen's legendary guitarist, is an astrophysicist, even though he could.

Instead, Hank puts his hands on my face and pulls me into him. We kiss once and then kiss more. We kiss as though we are stitched together, seamed by days and talks and wantings and getting it. His palms find their way to my waist, to my hair, and I can feel him smile as we kiss and as the music and night and ocean wash over us.

Everything ends: songs, summer, even kisses. But the best ones, the ones we mark with doodled lyrics or remembered chords, photographs and portraits, keep going, like the ocean here; rushing and easing, backing away and then returning. Like the song you need to hear at least one more time.

—